BROODY BRIT

USA TODAY Bestselling author
NAIMA SIMONE

OLIVERHEBERBOOKS

To Gary. 143.

To Connie Butts.
I'll miss you forever and love you longer than that.

CHAPTER 1

ZENOBIA

'm not a Taylor Swift fan.

Honestly? She can go kick rocks with bare-ass feet and a fresh pedicure. Granted, a good part of my enmity is mostly due to the fact that she got to do the nasty beast with two backs with Tom Hiddleston. From the way that man dances, I just know he can make a woman orgasm so hard, she's granted access to the universe and all its secrets. No doubt Taylor Swift knows what lies at the end of a black hole and if alien life-forms truly exist on Pluto.

Yeah, I can't stand her.

And yet, even I, the anti-Swiftie, can't deny that this new song is catchy as hell.

Good thing there's no one here to witness my defection as I pseudo-twerk while whisking eggs for my omelet. Don't worry, my girls over at Wonderland. Your pole is safe from me.

With the music on full blast, eggs and bacon at the ready and grits already simmering—yes, grits. I'm Providence, Rhode Island born and bred, but my grandmother is straight from The Country, Virginia—this is a good morning. And in the last month, those have been few and far between. So rare, they should probably be logged in on the endangered species list.

If anyone had told me eight weeks ago that I would be single, homeless, and the emotional equivalent of a Tasmanian devil with a crack problem, I would've checked their temperature—with a rectal thermometer and no gel. My life hasn't been perfect—whose is? But it'd been settled, secure, and dammit, mine.

But then, one morning, I arrived home to the apartment I shared with James, my boyfriend of three years. I'd just endured after a brutal sixteen-hour shift in Memorial Hospital's ER because of a pileup on Interstate 95 near Thurbers Avenue. But instead of sympathy or even a hot cup of coffee, my steady, reliable man had been hurriedly packing his clothes. Between the time I'd left for work and walked through the door the next day, he'd suffered an existential crisis and realized he wasn't ready to tie himself down in a committed relationship. He needed to "discover what awaited him out in the world", and he couldn't go all Lewis and Clark with me.

Apparently, what awaited him hadn't been that difficult to find. He hadn't needed to explore any farther than the third-floor Obstetrics department where Jenna, a bubbly, blonde nurse, worked. James and Jenna. That shit sounds like they should be hosting their own HGTV show on flipping foreclosed houses. In the time it'd taken him to stuff his teeth whitener and Rogaine in his suitcase, he'd moved in with her, casting me into the role of scorned woman in Memorial's answer to *Grey's Anatomy*.

Well, James might be a doctor, but he's sure as hell isn't a McDreamy.

McFuckboy, is more like it. God, I hate that I'm so bitter...

Taylor shuts off mid-Oh-oh.

"Bloody. Fucking. Hell." A low, rumbled growl punches me in the gut.

Fear barrels through me, hot, oil slick and stunning. For a moment, I stand there, frozen. Images from every crime show I've ever watched on the Investigation Discovery channel flash through my head like disco strobe lights.

Oh hell no.

Damn if somebody's going to cut me up and bury the parts under a newly poured concrete back deck without me going down fighting.

Snatching up two eggs from the carton, I spin around and hurl the produce at him like a grenade launcher. Without waiting to see where they land, I twist back to the stove and snatch up the steaming saucepan by the black handle.

"Hot grits, bitch. And I'm not afraid to use them. Better ask Al Green," I snap, tightening my grip on the handle even though the heat is stinging my hand without the pot holder.

The first thing I notice is the yellow glide of yolk down a wide, powerful, tattooed, *naked* chest. My eyes track the path between rock hard pecs, down a Photoshopped ladder of corrugated abs—because surely those don't exist in nature—and over the dangerously low band of gray sweatpants clinging valiantly to a slim pair of hips. My would-be murderer is fucking jacked.

Raising the pot higher, my gaze lifts up, up, up, and *uuup* to

Oh my God.

A Viking.

Fierce. The word bursts into my mind, booming like a cannon shot. A severe face of harsh, razor sharp angles and bold planes. Forget stone. Those cheekbones, the blade of his nose, and the solid line of his jaw could've been chiseled from the thickest sheet of ice. A person could risk frostbite attempting to stroke those features. Especially with those arctic-blue eyes trained on you in a glare that doesn't exactly invite a person to come within five feet, much less touch. But then there's that mouth. I swallow, my hold on the grits momentarily wavering before I add my other hand to steady it. Good Lord, that bottom-heavy mouth, with its just-shy-of-too-lush and totally cruel slant, could convince someone into considering if maybe losing a digit or two might be worth testing the juxtaposition of hard and soft. Worth a hands-on experiment of how long they can sustain the burn of the elicit promise inherent in those brutal yet carnal lips.

I suck in a breath and shift back a step. For more room to swing the contents of the pan, I convince myself. When in truth, we—me and the Viking—both know it's a retreat. Again, my pride works overtime, trying to persuade me it's because of his size, his brute strength. Not the overwhelming sexuality that exudes like a damn pheromone from every muscle, every inch of golden, inked skin—hell, every pore. No, not that.

"I don't know what grits"—that beautiful mouth sneers around the word—"are, but it can't be worse than that shit you're blasting at what the fuck in the morning."

The "bloody" should've tipped me off. But now, hearing him speak for a second time, recognition slams into me. Dr. Julian Arliss, my best friend Gabrielle's husband—and owners of the house I'm currently staying in—possesses a smooth, crisp and polished tone. This guy's voice is all grit and gravel, and yet lyrical. Different, but the accent is unmistakable. Utterly British.

Slowly, I lower the pot and my aching arms heave a sigh of relief that has my muscles quivering. Without removing my narrowed stare from him, I twist and set the grits on the stove. Once more, slower, I study the Viking's features. That similar but different accent is the only thing in common with Julian. This man's hair is blond, a darker shade, and even in my most apple martini-induced dreams, I couldn't envision Memorial's resident Dr. McSteamy sporting that mohawk. Or the tattoos that seem to cover every available inch of skin, including his hands and neck. And this man's gaze is bright like the purest heart of a flame and almost hard to peer into. A physician, Julian's genial bedside manner and easy smile aren't just for show; it's his personality. Not this guy. If Viking has a bedside manner, it's fuck 'em and leave 'em with a scowl for the poor soul daring to linger.

And yet, somehow, I can't see that woman harboring any regrets about being under that big body, even if her ass is covered in rug burn for being kicked out so quickly.

No. This Viking doesn't bear a resemblance to our much loved Dr. Arliss. But what're the chances that a British murderer would break into his countryman's house in the same suburb outside of Providence, Rhode Island? Unless, God switched the celestial channel of my life and instead of living in Meredith Grey's world, I'm now smack dab in a Lifetime movie? Nil.

"Okay," I concede, crossing my arms and leaning a hip against the counter. "So maybe you're not here to make a Stella McCartney original out of my skin." His frown devolves into a full out scowl that, *whew*, should not have my ovaries erupting into a flash mob. "From the accent, I'm assuming you know Julian, but I still... Who are you?"

"I could ask you the same question. Other than your dodgy taste in music and faulty decisions in wearing *that* to cook bacon, I don't know who the hell you are either."

That? Slowly, I straighten, my eyebrows lowering to match his scowl. Irritation rolls through me, and I refuse to glance down. Dodgy—whatever the hell that means—taste? Faulty decisions? Last time I checked, my twenty-eight-year-old ass didn't need his permission or approval. I've managed to eat, tie my shoes and become a nurse all by myself for a long time without his input, and I don't need his Judgy McJudgerson opinion now. Especially since I still don't know. Who. He. Is.

I part my lips, ready to tell him where he can shove his attitude with explicit directions of how hard, when the words shrivel up on my tongue along with the breath in my lungs.

That fire-and-ice gaze roams over my face as if exploring it, scouting the terrain for... What? I have no idea, but my instincts scream at me to shore up any wayward thoughts that might leak through my expression, my eyes. To risk giving nothing, because this man will pick up on it, use it… His scrutiny drops to my mouth, and the struggle to maintain my "I don't have two fucks to rub together" demeanor experiences a crisis. A crisis brought on by the unblinking, way-too-intense perusal that lingers on my lips then lowers to my breasts, my stomach that isn't anywhere as tight as his, my "child-bearing hips," as my grandmother called them, and thighs bared by the sleep shorts that just cover my ass.

My nipples bead into taut points, and not even Jesus Christ soaring down on a seraphim-enshrouded chariot could make me uncross my arms. Not when my ill-timed, unwanted and inappropriate reaction to a wide, strong pair of shoulders and thicker-than-tree-trunks thighs are on vivid display.

Damn. I knew I should've taken that nurse from Oncology up on his pity fuck in the on-call room. Pride made me turn him down, but standing here in Julian and Gabrielle's kitchen, I'm thinking hating myself a little would've been better than this guy knowing my body was hard up.

"*I* belong here," I snap. "That's who I am. Julian and Gabrielle invited me to stay here. They never mentioned you."

My overactive imagination conjures a flicker of… something in his glacial gaze. It's there and gone so quick, it must've been a reflective glint from the overhead lights. 'Cause there's no softer emotion in those eyes.

"And yet, here I am," he grunts, opening his muscular

arms wide. I try not to ogle him. I mean, I valiantly try. But there's just so damn *much* of him. "And I'm fair fucking knackered, so if you'd cut back on the ear-splitting noise first thing in the morning, that would be great, yeah?"

Oh no. That's not a request. It's an order, and it raises every hackle when I didn't even know I owned a hackle. But by now, I'm probably resembling a scorched cat. One ready to hiss and claw, and goddamn it yes, climb, that man. I don't care how brutally beautiful he is; no one dictates my movements or decisions. Not since I was sixteen.

My chest clenches, and I have to breathe through the spasm. Not now. Inhaling, I trap the air in my lungs for ten seconds, then release it slowly, deliberately. Beating back the memories, the *grief* that would swallow me whole like Jonah's whale if I allowed it.

"Listen… you. This must be some kind of misunderstanding or, I don't know, a double booking. But until we get this straightened out with Julian and Gabrielle, how about you go back to wherever you just climbed out of. And this is my territory over here. We can stay in our neutral corners."

And by "straightened out," I mean, get my best friend and her husband to kick this guy's ass out. As if James's defection wasn't enough of a bitch slap from the universe, my toilet decided to pull an *Exorcist*. Maybe the john didn't spin around, but it did vomit shit. With a diagnosis of busted pipes and an edict to abandon the premises for at least two weeks, I'm without a home. And shelling out money to stay half a month in a hotel was out of the question. Thank God Gabrielle opened her home to me since she, Julian, and the kids were all going to the happiest place on earth for vacation. With the suburb where she lives being only a ten-minute drive from Providence and the hospital where we work, my friends and their house are a godsend.

Their place—it's my sanctuary when my life has literally gone to shit. I promise, this guy doesn't need it as badly as I do.

So, I'm not going anywhere. But him…

"I can see those wheels turning, Swiftie. And I hate to break it to you, but I'm not going anywhere. That apartment is mine for the next four months, so if anyone's ass is going to leave skid marks on that pretty, paved driveway, it's going to be yours."

He didn't… Oh hell no… That's not… Apartment?

"I am. Not a. Swiftie," I grind out. *Oh shit.* That's my comeback. *That's my damn comeback.* I need coffee. *Stat.* And him out of my space.

He snorts, one of his thick, brown eyebrows arching.

"You know what?" I snap, turning around and snatching up my neglected bowl of eggs and fork. "Back to your apartment, cave, or bridge. Whatever fits."

Relative or friend of Julian's or not, he's an ass. A grumpy ass. And I'm through talking to him.

"You're no fucking Prince Harry," I grumble, whisking as if my life depends on it. His might.

"And you're no goddamn duchess," he shoots back. "Cheers, pet."

I whip around, a retort burning my tongue like a poker, but it's extinguished. Because he's walking away and damn him for looking as good leaving as he did coming.

Nonono. Scratch that. Don't think of him, that giant body flat on a bed, back arched, thighs straining with that big hand wrapped around an equally big cock. Coming.

Dammit.

I hate myself.

This is all Taylor Swift's fault.

CHAPTER 2

xel. His name is Axel Wright.

It's gritty. Unique. A little bit dirty.

Sexy as hell.

In other words, it fits the grumpy giant from the kitchen.

I scowl out the windshield of my car toward the ER entrance as if it's at fault for the Viking's perfect name. And deliciousness.

"Z, I'm so sorry I forgot to tell you about Axel staying at the house," Gabrielle apologizes in a hushed voice.

The high-pitched squeals and laughter of children swell for a minute in the background before the quiet click echoes over the phone line and silence replaces the carefree, joyous noise.

"Whew," she breathes on a huff, and I can easily imagine her sweeping her pretty brown locs back from her face. "I love my family. Adore them, and every day I have to pinch myself to make sure this is my life. But I can't lie. A teen and four-year-old twins hopped up on Disney euphoria? I swear, I want to test every soda and hot dog to see if they're secretly slipping kids speed. They haven't stopped going since we arrived."

She blows out another gust of air and it ends on a small chuckle.

"Julian volunteered to take Xavier, Cecee, and Bree down to the beach. Something tells me he's angling for sex later. And considering how grateful I am right now, he's going to get some."

"I'm so glad I work at a hospital so I can use the industrial strength bleach to cleanse my brain of that image," I grumble. "Please keep your hedonistic hijinks to yourself. Especially since I work with your husband *and* I'm currently stuck in a sexual drought."

"My bad, Z." Gabrielle snickers and doesn't sound the least bit remorseful for my neglected and forsaken lady parts. "And I really am sorry about Axel. He was supposed to arrive a few weeks ago, but changed his mind. Julian didn't find out until last night that Axel had arrived in the States—when he called from the airport. He'd better be glad we're bad homeowners and left the spare key under the fake rock," she grumbles. "Anyway, I haven't met him yet, but Julian did mention he's a bit… rough around the edges. Did everything go okay?"

I glance down at my watch. Ten minutes before my two o'clock shift starts. Not nearly enough time to regale her with my disastrous meeting with her mysterious houseguest.

"Fine," I lie, Axel's biting "duchess" ringing in my ears hours later. "He just caught me by surprise. I wasn't expecting a real-life Viking to suddenly appear in the kitchen while I was cooking breakfast." I leave out the threat of splashing him with hot grits.

Gabrielle's bark of laughter rings in my ear. "A Viking? Oh, I have to tell Julian that one." She snickers again. "Like I said, I haven't met him yet, but I have seen pictures. And yes, I'm a happily married woman with a beautiful husband. But damn. That man is hot. Like, virile, primal, gorgeous hot."

Annoyance flashes through me at the dreamy note that enters her voice, and I immediately slap it down. What the hell is that? All three of those blind mice could see Axel is beautiful in the way of a large, stalking lion—commanding, wild, stunning, and dangerous as hell. Why should it matter if Gabrielle, of all people, should notice? Or anyone, for that matter.

Nope, it doesn't matter, and the quicksilver spike of irritation must be a result of the coffee I never did manage to drink.

Note to self: stock Gabrielle's house with morning blend K-cups before I hurt somebody.

"If you like that type," I hedge, realizing Gabrielle had fallen quiet. "Who is he anyway?" I ask her the question that has been plaguing me since turning around to watch egg yolk slide off his chest. Damn lucky egg yolk. "I didn't notice a familial resemblance between him and Julian."

"Obviously, they're not blood-related, but Julian considers Axel family just the same." She sighs, and unconsciously, I curl my fingers around my steering wheel and lean forward. There's a story here, and while my brain screams that I shouldn't be this interested in it, my increasingly racing pulse begs to differ.

Curiosity. It's normal to be curious about the man I'm apparently going to be sharing a house with for the next two weeks.

"Axel is the younger brother of Julian's childhood best friend, Blake. They grew up together in England, and they, along with Trish—you remember Trish, right? My friend, the yoga instructor?"

I nod, even though Gabrielle can't see the gesture. I'd attended a couple of the British woman's classes along with Gabrielle, but quickly determined all that stretching and posing and *hurting* wasn't my thing. She's cool people, though.

"When they were sixteen, the three of them were on vacation at Trish's family's lake house in Scotland. They snuck out one night and decided to take one of the boats onto the lake. There were only two life jackets, and Blake insisted Julian and Trish wear them since he was the better swimmer."

Dread coils in my stomach, congealing into a hard knot. Oh God. I know where this is heading, and part of me wants to interrupt Gabrielle and tell her never mind. But the words lodge in my constricted throat, and my grip tightens on the cell phone.

Her voice drops, and it's barely above a whisper. "When the water became choppy, they were far out in the middle of the lake. The boat capsized, and Blake went under. Julian tried to find him, to save him, but he couldn't. The authorities found Blake's body three days later."

"Oh Jesus," I whisper. Unbidden, an image of a younger

Julian diving over and over beneath dark, rough waters, searching for his friend wavered in front of my eyes. I can't imagine... An instant later, that picture shifts and Axel replaces it. Axel as he'd been this morning. The frown. That flash of emotion that I believed had been a fracture of light.

I understand oh too intimately how loss could harden you, embitter you. Isolate you. Grief... I shake my head, briefly closing my eyes. It can slowly take you apart, memory by memory, organ by organ, cell by cell. And when you're reforged, the person staring back at you from the mirror is unrecognizable. It'll change how you live life. Or not live it. Time doesn't matter, doesn't lessen the pain. Not if you've spent the years hoarding that pain like old magazines. Pulling them out, flipping through them, indulging in them.

"Yeah," Gabrielle continued. "As you can imagine, Julian took Blake's death hard, and it affected him. But he still remained in contact with Axel, who was twelve when his brother died. According to Julian, Axel changed, withdrew into himself and from everyone else. And he buried himself in his art."

Shock ricochets through me. "Art?"

"Oh God, yes," Gabrielle says, and though she's mentioned several times that she's never formally met Axel, I can't miss the note of pride that warms her voice. "He's incredible, Z. You should see some of the things he's created. Axel works mainly with metal, and he sculpts the most amazing pieces. He's gained a name in England and has started to become known over here in the States. That's what he's here for, actually. His first New York gallery opening. It's four months away in February, and Julian insisted he stay with us while he worked on the pieces for his show."

Okay, this is… a lot. An avalanche of information, and at the forefront streams a movie reel of Axel, long hair of his mohawk contained in a bun, shirtless, tatted skin smudged with oil and soot, muscles straining as he pounds metal into shape. As he applies a torch to iron, welding it into his own creation like a modern-day Hephaestus.

The image is pure ridiculousness; no sane person would work around such hazardous equipment without a shirt or a helmet. But try as I might, I can't evict the fantasy. Can't stop the slow spiral of heat that winds its way through my veins, leaving my breasts heavy and sensitive, clenching my belly and pooling between my thighs. I squirm on my driver's seat. Please, God, don't let anyone walk past. Me, in scrubs and in heat.

Not a good look.

"It sounds like he's going to be super busy, so I guess that means we won't see that much of each other. Living together for the next couple of weeks should be easy peasy." Super busy. Easy peasy. God, when I lie, I turn into freaking Pollyanna.

"Thanks, babe," Gabrielle sighs. "And again, I'm sorry for not giving you the proper heads-up. I better go save Julian. I mean, join him. Join him." She snorted. "Take care of yourself and have a great shift, okay?"

Code: don't junk punch James.

Not that I would. He, Jenna, and their fixer-upper show aren't worth the job I love and worked my ass off to get. But damn. A girl can dream.

"I will. Enjoy yourself."

We end the call, and minutes later, I enter the hospital and clock in. The next few hours fly by in a blur of asthma attacks, stitches, broken bones, fevers, and one brain aneurysm that's rushed off to Neurology. It's hectic, organized chaos, and busy enough that I barely have time to complete a chart before another case is rushed in.

Some days, the ER is slow like a lull in a storm. Other days, it's like a battlefield. It's never boring, never the same. It isn't for the faint of heart.

And I love it.

Watching my grandmother suffer from diabetes—standing by helpless as first her toes, then foot, then leg was taken—might have spurred my desire—no, need—to become a nurse. But it's the love of people, of helping where I can and offering comfort where I can't, that keeps me here.

"I'm about to go get dinner before another wave hits. You want me to bring you something back?" Julia, another nurse, asks as she rounds the desk I'm slumped behind.

"No, I brought mine with me. But thanks."

"No problem. I won't be long." She smiles, but as she turns, her expression darkens. Her swift glance at me holds traces of anger, embarrassment and… pity.

It's the pity that burns like acid poured over an open wound.

It's also pity that clues me in on what—or who—I will see when I turn around. And like a masochist, I twist in my chair, bracing myself. But humiliation has a way of corroding the toughest and thickest of shields.

And my defenses might as well as be constructed of paper-mache as I stare at my ex and his new girlfriend.

I should look away. Suddenly become engrossed with paperwork or charts. Hell, go troll for patients. But I can't move. Can't tear my gaze away from the happy couple. Can't stop my chest from constricting as he pinches her chin and smiles down at her like he used to do to me so often through the three years we were together.

Unoriginal bastard.

He could *at least* find a new PDA gesture. I bet he does the same kiss-pinch nipple-missionary-style combo with her in bed, too. I should feel sorry for her...

Naaah.

"What are either of them doing down here anyway?" Julia sneered.

"We had someone come in on a possible suicide attempt. Dr. Graham called James down for a psych eval," I explained, deliberately turning around and facing her again. "And Jenna?"

I shrug, grasping for a nonchalance that didn't exist.

"She's here to see her man."

"Zenobia, I can stay here if you want to go eat dinner," Julia murmurs. There's that awful sympathy again in her gaze and voice, and it's all I can do not to yell, *Stop. I'm not fragile. I'm not pathetic.*

Even if I berate myself for being both of those things in the darkest part of the night while I lie in my best friend's guest room.

"No." I smile, and throw in a shooing motion, just because. "That's all right. I'm all right. Now get outta here. I heard one of the doctors mention they have okra on the dinner menu tonight."

I force a laugh as Julia scrunches her face into a disgusted moue.

"I know how much you love it."

And her let-me-watch-the-bitch-just-in-case-she-leaps-over-the-desk eyes are making me itchy. I mean, she's not *wrong*. But still… itchy.

"Right." She studies me for a moment longer before tapping the top of the desk. "I won't be long."

"I'll be here," I shoot back.

She disappears down the hall, and I exhale a long, hard breath. Okay, I'm an adult. A full grown one. I can handle being cordial to my cheating ex and my replacement. Not a problem.

"Hey, Zenobia."

I squeeze my eyes shut and control the wave of panic and anger that spasms inside me. *You can't throw syringes at him like darts. You can't throw syringes at him like darts.* It's unreasonable, if you ask me. Obviously, whoever in HR came up with the rules never had a douchebag ex.

"James," I greet, giving my chair an unhurried spin. "Jenna." I nod at the blonde who looks like she would rather be elbow deep in an expectant mom's vagina than standing here with her new man in front of his old girlfriend.

I'm so sorry she's uncomfortable. Unfortunately, I had a freshly baked batch of fucks to give this morning, but now I'm all out.

Sigh. Damn, that was bitchy.

James squints and runs a hand over his hair, and I bite my tongue to trap the snarky reminder of how that speeds up thinning. Not true, but I think God will forgive me the little lie. Instead, I meet his gaze with an unwavering stare of my own. He repeats the nervous gesture, and I take no mercy on him by breaking the silence. I didn't ask him to come over here and be polite. Fuck polite. Polite can go get gang-banged like an adult star on Pornhub.

He clears his throat. "So, I—"

My cell buzzes against my hip. Relief blasts through me so hard. My stomach seizes, and I shoot up a finger, reaching for my phone. "Hold that thought." But a glance down at the name on the screen, and excitement edged in fear replaces the relief. My heart slams hard against my sternum and then races. Almost lightheaded, I surge to my feet, phone clutched in my numb fingers. "Excuse me. I need to take this."

Not waiting for either of them to reply, I stride away from the desk, signaling to another nurse that I need a moment. With trembling fingers, I press the screen and lift the phone to my ear.

"Hey, Sabrina." I close in on the nearest on-call room and charge in. A swift scan reveals it's empty and thank God. Whatever she's is calling to tell me, I don't relish an audience for it. "How're you doing?"

"I'm fine, Z. Busy today?" Sabrina Lorenzo replies, her warm tone that I equate with kindness and compassion echoing in my ear. But today, nothing can pierce the cacophony of emotions clashing and clanging in my chest, my head.

"It's been pretty non-stop, but..." I swallow, and the air whistles out of my lungs. "Have you—" My voice is almost soundless, a whisper of the painful anticipation ricocheting inside me. I swallow again. Try again. "Have you heard anything from the Mavises?"

Sabrina doesn't immediately reply, but we've been together since I was sixteen years old. First, when I, pregnant and scared, met with her to discuss adoption. We started as counselor and client, where she guided and supported me through the semi-open adoption process. She held my hand after I turned my baby girl over to Gregory and Danielle Mavis after holding her only once. Inhaling her baby scent that even twelve years later, I can still smell. She sat with me, comforted me, laughed with me when I received pictures of and updates on Bethany from Greg and Danielle. Through emails and digital images, I've watched my little girl thrive and grow. And Sabrina has been with me every step of the way. And now, years later, I count Sabrina as a friend, as family.

And, so, when she doesn't say anything, I interpret that unspoken words in that silence.

Burning grief and fanged disappointment burrow so deep into my heart and soul that I'm unable to smother the gasp of pain. I press my hand to my chest, fingers splayed wide. But nothing can contain the hurt, the grief. It's pouring out of me with every sluggish beat of my heart, and as I glance down, I'm partially shocked to not see it coating my scrubs, my skin.

"Z," Sabrina says, her voice gentle but firm. It barely penetrates the crimson, pulsing haze surrounding me. "Z, I want you to listen to me. This is just a no, *for now*. They don't think it's a good time for you and Bethany to meet. When we sent the request, we knew this could be a possibility. But, honey, this doesn't mean they can't change their mind a year from now, even a month from now."

When I chose a semi-open adoption, I'd believed I was choosing the best course for all of us. My baby would have mature, loving parents who could provide for her emotionally and physically. She would have the time to bond with her new family without feeling confused or torn in two between her adoptive parents and me. And through letters and pictures, I could be a part of her life, witnessing her milestones and go on, buoyed by the knowledge that she was safe, protected and loved.

But I always had the promise that one day, when Greg and Danielle deemed it appropriate, I could meet Bethany face-to-face and get to know her. With my daughter about to enter her teens, I thought maybe they would agree to this being the time.

But no. And I ached with the disappointment, the emptiness of another year going by and my little girl not in my life.

"Did they say why?" I rasp.

"No, honey. They didn't," Sabrina murmurs. "I'm so sorry. I know how much you wanted this. We'll try again. Bethany's birthday is in another eight months. We'll approach them again and see if they feel differently."

"Okay."

I pinch the bridge of my nose, trying to shove back the tears that sting my eyes.

"Okay," I repeat, hating the quiver in my voice. Hating myself for hoping. I should've known better. "Listen, Sabrina, I need to go. It's been really busy and… and…"

"I understand, Z," she whispers. And for the third time

tonight, that fucking pity. I squeeze the bridge of my nose harder. It's either that or rage, scream… sob. "I'll talk to you later, okay? Call me tonight if you need me. I don't care how late."

"Will do," I answer briskly, needing to end this call. To immerse myself back in the chaos of the emergency room so I can't think. Can't break down.

I end the call and rush out of the on-call room back to the floor desk.

Back to my job, my calling.

All that I have left to call my own.

CHAPTER 3

New England Patriots. The Red Sox. The Boston Bruins. Or Brutes.

Fuck if I know 'em. Or care to. Yeah, American football teams have played over in England a few times, but as much as the US would like for it to catch on, sorry, mate. It's just not going to happen. It's annoying as hell that they keep trying. It's Leeds United or fuck off.

Since Nate Granger is the guy Julian hired to drive me around Providence—or at least until I learn to drive myself since I'm not some old nob—I'll keep my opinion about his inferior football to myself. It's best not to piss him off too soon. Especially when I still need him.

"Just let me know if you want to come over this Sunday for the game, Ax," Nate offers, as excited as a puppy. I'm half surprised his arse isn't wiggling on the seat. He's a younger guy, about twenty-two. And even though he talks too damn much, he's a nice kid. Which is the only reason I don't snap at him to not call me fucking Ax. "Me and the guys get together to watch the Pats play, and we wouldn't mind one more. We'll grill out, drink some beers. It'll be fun."

My balls might've actually crawled up into my gut at the invitation.

Get-togethers. People. Talking. On their own, they send shivers charging down my spine in a death march. Together?

Oh fuck no.

Thankfully, he pulls up in front of Julian's house, and as soon as Nate shifts the gear into park, I shove on the passenger side door and damn near leap out. It's indecent, and I should be embarrassed with how fast I'm out of the truck and rounding the hood. But then I think of him issuing another invite, and yeah, I'm good with being a coward.

"Cheers, mate," I call out, flicking a wave as I head toward the separate entrance to the in-law apartment off the main house.

"Mate. Hah! That's so cool!" Nate cackles. "See you tomorrow, mate!"

Shaking my head, I lift my arm in another wave. Why do I get the feeling that he's going to be calling me that from now on? Oh well. Better than Ax.

Only one person used that shortened version of my name. And hearing it on the lips of anyone else is like railroad nails jammed into my chest.

With a beep of his horn, Nate pulls off, the loud engine of his truck fading, and the quiet of the neighborhood sinks in. I jerk to a stop in front of the side door, my key hovering meters from the lock. Closing my eyes, I inhale, hold my breath. Seconds later, I release it, but a wave of longing crashes into me, catching me unaware and damn near knocking me on my arse.

The only thing this place has in common with my cottage back in Ilkey is the quiet. And even that's different. Here, it's a noisier silence, one pockmarked by the muted shouts of children, the distant promise of traffic, the knowledge that a congested city lurks not too far off.

I crave the softer silence. The tickle of wind, the patter of rain and droning hum of cicadas. The faint ringing of bells at All Saints Parish Church on Sunday mornings. Even the smell differs. This air isn't a hodgepodge of grass, storm-heavy clouds, and the faintly acidic soil of Ilkey Moor.

Fuck. How big a mistake did I make coming here? I didn't go into art for the fame or the money. I did it for my peace, my soul. My sanity. And right now, I'm resenting the hell outta Julian for convincing me to let it be more than that. For chasing more. I don't want more.

All I want is to be left alone.

Sighing, I jab the key into the lock and twist harder than necessary. First, shower. Then food. Maybe I can find a good place within walking distance to get some take-away.

I toss everything in my pockets on the small bedside table—change, wallet, inhaler—then strip as I cross the small apartment and enter the bathroom. Seconds later, water hot enough to scald pours down over me. I'm not as sweaty or grimy as I would've been if I'd worked on any pieces, because I'd spent a good part of the day trolling a couple of junkyards.

The therapist Mum and Dad sent me to after Blake died

would've had a field day with the knowledge that I fish through rubbish to save it for my work. If I'd opened up to her, that is. I hadn't. Because that would've required talking.

Without my permission, an image of the woman from the kitchen barges into my head. I hadn't seemed to have a problem talking to her this morning. Of course, being threatened with a pan of hot, white, lumpy shit would probably loosen up any man's tongue.

"Zenobia," I quietly say, trying out her name aloud. Rolling my tongue around it, tasting. Julian had said her name was Zenobia Hester.

For such a little person, she was fierce as hell. Even egg sliding down my chest couldn't keep me from noticing the light brown and gold of her narrowed eyes. The echo of that godawful shit she called music still ringing in my ears couldn't distract me from the almost arrogant slopes of her cheekbones or the patrician slant of her nose with its wide nostrils. And nothing God had managed to create in six days could divert my attention from that damn near indecent dick tease of a mouth. Plush like the softest of down pillows. Sinful like the souls of a packed Sunday service. I don't think I've ever seen something that beautiful yet lewd.

But then, my gaze hadn't slid down to that curvy, ripe, tight body yet.

Christ.

Standing in that kitchen with her murdering me in about eleven different ways with her glare, I'd had to think of walking in on my parents having sex when I was nine. My mate Rory Dunn's sixth toe. Old man Johnson's penchant for watering his garden naked. Fucking anything that would convince my cock not to rise like a goddamn flagpole.

Helen of Troy's face launched a thousand ships. This woman's body could launch a thousand dicks.

Breasts that had my palms itching to cup, squeeze... fuck. Oh, damn right, too easily I could imagine straddling her chest and sliding my hard, throbbing flesh between those perfect tits. And if God really existed, then that wicked mouth would greet my cock, welcoming it. Swallowing it. A nipped in waist that my big hands could effortlessly span flaring into gorgeous, wide hips. My fingers curl into my palms, as if forbidding me to grab ahold of that flesh even in my filthy fantasies. Refusing to let me test and see how hard I could grip before it bruised. Not that I would mind marking that gorgeous, brown skin. Wouldn't mind her looking in a mirror as I am now and seeing them, knowing I'd put them there. And she'd craved it.

Then there were those thick thighs and miracle of an arse. A man would find himself in heaven cradled between those strong, rounded legs and be consigned to hell when he clutched the flagrant curves of her arse. One glance and the insatiable urge to touch could transform a man into an animal or a supplicant.

I've been both for my art. Never for a woman.

And I don't plan on turning over a new leaf now.

Besides, she seems like the kind of woman who would demand flowers, fine meals, and even finer conversation. Yeah, that ain't me. Hurried fucks against a pub wall that only require a shifting of clothes and a condom—that's more my speed.

Not many words and no commitment required.

I finish up my shower and quickly dry off, securing the towel around my waist and slicking my hair back. Snatching another towel off the rack with probably more force than necessary, I scrub it over my head, shoulders and chest. I'm here in America now. There's no turning back, and all my focus needs to be on creating the pieces for this art show in four months. Then I can go back home.

To my life.

To my solitude.

Wrapping the cloth around my waist, I exit the loo and head back into the room that makes up most of what Julian called a mother-in-law flat. It's small, but I don't give a fuck about the size. It suits my needs just fine. A bed big enough to fit me, a desk, closet, tall dresser for my clothes, and a bedside table for everything else. Then the door that leads to the garage and a separate entrance to the kitchen. Yeah, not thinking about the kitchen or the woman who's occupying the rest of the house...

My phone vibrates, jumping slightly against the wood of the desk. Frowning, I switch direction from the bed and head over to it. Not many people call me. My agent, the owners of the junkyards I haunt to let me know when a new load has arrived, and since deciding to come to America, Julian has shown up in my missed calls more often. I talked to my agent this morning and Julian last night. Pete and Bert are aware I'm not home.

Which leaves only two people.

My parents.

Shit.

Guilt punches me in the chest. If I were any kind of son

—the kind of son they want and deserve—dread wouldn't swirl and churn in my gut at the sight of the steadily buzzing phone. Tight bands wouldn't squeeze my torso like a vise, restricting my air. No. No worthy son would react that way to just a phone call from his mother or father.

But then, I'm nowhere near worthy.

Nowhere near the son they desire… or lost.

Clenching my jaw, I grab the cell, and with a cursory glance at the name on the screen, jab the answer button and haul the phone to my ear.

"Hello, Mum."

"Axel," she greets in that cool, posh tone she's never lost, although she's lived farther north with my firmly middle-class father for over thirty years.

It never ceases to amaze me that my upper-class mother fell in love with a medical student and gave up her wealthy life in the "more civilized south" to reside in Leeds. Still, she'd planned for her children to eventually become doctors or solicitors. Blake had been intended to follow in our father's footsteps. Who knows what might've happened if he'd lived? Maybe he and Julian would've opened a practice together. Or maybe not. We've never spoken about it, but part of me believes Julian went into medicine because of Blake's death.

Every hope of my becoming my father's son died when I shit on that dream by not even attending uni. Mum bricked it when I announced that bit of information. Both her and Dad did. But her especially. She'd considered my withdrawal into art a hobby, not a passion or a lifeline. Definitely not a career. But when I told her I was going into welding instead of school, I think that was the day she gave up on me. Doesn't matter that I'm gaining some fame as an artist or that my sculptures have been exhibited in lobbies of the poshest buildings in Leeds City Centre, have been a part of shows at The Tetley and the Henry Moore Institute, or that some of the wealthiest men in England have commissioned pieces for their homes or offices. No, none of that matters.

I'm not who she imagined Blake would one day be.

"What are you doing up so late?" It's after twelve in England, though she has no idea I'm here in the States. Closing my eyes, I pinch the bridge of my nose. Hopefully, this conversation will go better than our previous... hundreds. "Is everything okay?"

"Yes, fine." She releases a small sigh and I easily picture her waving off my question and concern with a flick of her fingers. "Your father was called to hospital for a long-time patient of his. Besides, I knew with how you work, this would be a good time to reach you. How has your asthma been? Are you being careful? I've said it before, working in that workshop surrounded by all that metal and chemicals cannot be good for your health."

Such familiar ground—both the inquisition about my healthcare precautions and the gripes over my career.

"Yeah, I've been staying on top of the asthma. I just had an appointment with my doctor. Oxygen levels good. Steroid inhaler is managing it well, and he renewed my prescription for the emergency one as well. All good, Mum."

Shit, I've only been dealing with the respiratory disease since I was a young'n. It's been three years since an attack landed me in the hospital with pneumonia. Nothing I could've done to prevent it; with asthma, shit happens, and the shitty, wet British weather doesn't help. Of course, I could've gone to hospital as soon as it felt like a damn anvil sat on my chest. But I didn't, and I haven't heard the end of it yet.

This thing—the disease, my lungs—always leaves me feeling defective. Weak. I didn't play football with other kids. I didn't run around the playground with them. I couldn't because too strenuous exercise of any kind could set off a coughing and wheezing attack. So, I withdrew into my art. It was my friend and never made me feel frail or different. When I got older and my parents couldn't dictate my actions, I started working out, got into mixed martial arts, though I never fought professionally, and went into a career where the appropriate precautions mean the difference between life and death. Literally.

Yeah, neither of my parents is happy with my choices.

But living by their rules and their expectations could also mean death for me. Maybe not physically, but definitely emotionally, mentally.

Still, as her question came from a place of concern, I keep the irritation out of my tone. Barely.

"That's good. I'm glad you're taking your health seriously, Axel." She pauses. "Especially with you nowhere near your doctor since you're in the United States and didn't see fit to disclose this to your parents."

Fuck.

"Can you explain to me why I had to find out about this relocation out of the country from Julian?"

Jesus.

Pinching the bridge of my nose—hard—I tip my head

back, open my mouth and silently yell to the ceiling. *Fuuuuuck.*

My parents and I talk so rarely that, sadly, it didn't occur to me to call and inform them about my show here in Rhode Island.

"Sorry, Mum," I grumble, suddenly feeling like a disobedient young'n caught in a lie. Whether the lie is being sorry I didn't tell her or that Julian *did*—yeah, I don't know. Either one makes me a complete shit. "I forgot."

I didn't think you'd give a damn.

I didn't want to hear your indifference.

I desperately want you to care and be proud of me and didn't think my soul could take another blow when you did neither.

But I said none of those much too revealing declarations; my mother wouldn't have appreciated the vulgar display of emotion, and I wouldn't have appreciated the rejection.

So, "I forgot" would have to do as way of explanation.

She sighed, and its beleaguered *God what have I ever done to deserve such a son?* sentiment rang clear like a church bell on a Sunday morning calling worshippers to service. Can't blame her. Sometimes I ask myself—and God—the same question. Why take the wrong son? My parents would never admit it, but I'm sure they have asked themselves that. Blake... As brilliant, kind, and driven as he was, he would've changed the world. Even at sixteen, he'd been a force to be reckoned with.

Me? I'm not trying to take anything by storm. Finding a place to wait it out would do me just fine. Much to my agent's annoyance.

"So, when is *this show* supposed to happen?" she asks, the emphasis on "this show" along the same vein of "this root canal" or "this gynecological appointment." And fuck. Jesus. I need to bleach the thought of my mum in stirrups out of my bloody brain.

"Three months." *Don't ask. Don't you fucking ask.* "Think you and Dad can make it?"

You bleeding-heart bastard.

She sighs. And that's all the answer I need. Shit. I'm like a living punching bag when it comes to her. She delivers that jab, and I just swing back for more.

"I can't see that happening, Axel. You know your father can't leave his practice for any length of time. He has patients who depend on him."

"Yeah." I nod, scrubbing a hand down my face. "I have to go, Mum. I'll ring later, yeah?"

After hanging up, I drag on a pair of jeans and a white T-shirt. The neckline is stretched to hell and there's a hole near the hem, but hell, it's clean. That's pretty much all I require. Padding barefoot out of my apartment and through the connecting garage, I twist the knob on the kitchen entrance and enter the empty room.

Relief rushes through me in a cool cascade. After the phone call with Mum, I don't feel like encountering the prickly nurse who threatened me with a bowl of whatever-the-hell-grits-are. I shake my head and walk toward the huge, steel refrigerator. Still don't know if that white shit was supposed to be some kind of porridge—and I don't care to find out either. Some American things need to stay right fucking here on this side of the pond.

"Oh, good, you're here."

Tension shoots up my spine like the crackle of lightning, settling in my shoulders and buzzing in my head. I don't need to glance behind me to identify that voice. And not because there's only one other person living in this house with me. The instantaneous hardening of my cock and the almost painful clenching of my gut and chest clue me in on who just entered the kitchen. I close my eyes and just resist not tipping my head back and demanding God confesses to whatever the hell I'd ever done to Him to torture me like this.

Six months. That's how long it's been since I was last balls-deep in a woman. After my ex-girlfriend broke it off with me, I've been taking a hiatus from women. Up until I saw this woman standing in a kitchen with that gorgeous face and hot as fuck body, screwing my fist had been doing me just fine. I have a feeling my cock is going to rebel, and my fist is going on strike.

Traitorous bastards.

Dragging in a deep breath, I steel myself and slowly turn around.

And glimpse that beautiful arse bent over the kitchen table. Blue scrubs tighten over her firm, full flesh, and my fingers curl into my tingling palms at my thighs. Jesus fucking Christ. She's trying to kill me. Julian's the doctor, but I've never heard of death by blue balls. And it never seemed a possibility. Till now.

Julian had called me earlier while I was at the workshop and informed me who my new flatmate was, apologizing for forgetting to tell me about her emergency situation. Something to do with a flooded flat. He'd also assured me that her schedule as an emergency room nurse meant we wouldn't be running into each other too much.

Apparently, his definition of "too much" greatly differed from mine.

'Cause I was thinking more along the lines of not at all.

But here we are. Me ogling her arse like it's the bloody Mona Lisa, and her not even aware that I'm struggling not to be *that* arsehole who doesn't respect a woman's personal space. Or the right not to have a fucker's cock rubbed against her.

"I don't know if you've eaten yet, but I stopped and bought Chinese food for dinner," she carries on, straightening from setting a couple of plastic bags on the table. With a deep, low groan that sounds way too carnal, she presses both hands to her lower back and stretches. Thrusting those gorgeous tits forward. The light blue top pulls across the mounds, highlighting the shape of them. Fueling every fantasy of how perfectly they would fit my hands. And I have big fucking hands.

Shit. She's definitely trying to kill me.

But I'm not above begging for a quick squeeze of that worship-worthy arse and those gorgeous tits before I meet my Maker.

"Axel?" She drops her arms and cocks her head, peering at me. "Did you hear me?"

"Yeah." I scrub a hand over my damp hair and down one shaved side of my head. "Chinese food. Cheers," I mutter and amble over to the table.

She huffs out a breath, and a wry smile curls one corner of her lush mouth. My fingers curl around one of the forks that spilled out of the bag, and the plastic bites into my palm. I welcome the tiny flair of pain. Anything to bank the tingle in my fingers. I recognize that herald of sensation. My fingers are itching to grab hold of a pencil and draw. Draw her face, a conglomeration of proud angles, regal slants and lascivious curves. As an artist, I'm fascinated by that face.

As a man, I want to fuck it.

"I had no idea what you would like, so I bought a bit of almost everything. Lo mein, sweet and sour pork, beef and peppers, shrimp egg foo young, fried rice and egg rolls. Some egg drop soup, too." She frowned, tapping a finger against bottom lip. "Well, damn. I hope you're not a vegetarian. But seriously, the kind of day I had calls for straight carnivore eating habits. When assholes be assholing, only meat will do."

She crosses the kitchen to one of the cabinets and removes a stack of paper plates while I'm staring at the mountain of takeaway containers, trying to decipher what the fuck she's talking about.

On a good day, words are a struggle. Not because I don't have them. In my head, they're there, streaming through my mind like a live news feed. But talking? To people? Yeah, not my thing. As a kid, I was shy, awkward, and kept to myself a lot. And after Blake… It just got worse. I didn't *want* to talk. Just wanted to be left alone, and I withdrew into my own world. Let my art speak for itself. What it had to say was much more eloquent and important than any words I could ever string together. They spoke from the soul, the heart.

"I'm Zenobia, by the way," she says, dropping the plates next to the bags. Her nose wrinkles, and she shoots a glance my way. "I thought we should start over considering our less than illustrious—and violent—meeting."

I snort, grabbing one of the containers. Without paying too much attention to what I'm piling on my plate—food's food—I mumble, "I know."

"You spoke with Julian and Gabrielle?" She winces, lowering into the chair across the table from me. "I guess we're going to be living together for the next two weeks. Sorry about this morning. I promise, no flying food for the next couple of weeks."

She smiles, holding her hand up, palm out. When I just stare at her, she slowly lowers it, her lips flattening.

"Well, anyway"—she shakes her head, reaching for the open carton of fried rice—"Gabrielle mentioned you're an artist and have your first New York show in a few months."

I nod.

"That has to be exciting."

Exciting? If she means in the way that standing up in front of a class bare arse naked is exciting, then yeah.

I hate gallery shows. Feeling like a glorified show pony on display. Waiting around and watching people judge not just you but your work. And the fucking talking. All people want to do is talk. *What was your inspiration? What's your process? Can I come watch you work? Tell me about this one...* It's fucking torture and my personal hell. But a necessary one, according to my agent who, for some unfathomable reason, hasn't dropped me as a client yet. Though, she's threatened to more times than I can remember. Who am I kidding? It's more likely the fact that my last commissioned piece went for twenty-k rather than my winning personality that keeps her around.

Continuing to shovel food in my mouth, I don't answer. No one ever wants to hear the truth anyway. Especially since I realize what an arsehole I'm being over it. How many artists would sell their soul and their arse to have this opportunity? And here I am complaining about it. Privilege at its worst.

"I don't know if Julian told you, but I work with them at the hospital. Which is how I ended up house-sitting—if you can really call it that. They're really taking pity on me because of a shitstorm at my apartment. True story."

She snickers, but there's a bitter edge to it that has curiosity jabbing its elbows into my sides, desperate to ask details about that enigmatic statement and the hint of resentment that's part and parcel with it. I fork more lo mein into my mouth.

"But my apartment should be cleaned and hopefully fumigated within an inch of its life in a couple of weeks. I assured her we could manage not to maim one another in that time. Besides, with my schedule and you working on the pieces for your show, we'll both be pretty busy and out of each other's hair."

Her gaze flicks to mine before lifting to take in said hair. And stays there. I clench my teeth and fingers, resisting the urge to restore some kind of order to the long strands that I didn't bother brushing or tying back after getting out of the shower.

I'm not fucking *preening*.

"Do you have a studio or workshop set up here?" she asks.

"Yeah."

She pauses, fork frozen midway to her mouth, as if waiting for me to continue. She's going to be waiting for a while. *Expounding* is not in my repertoire. After a few moments of silence stretched so thin it begs for mercy, she frowns, then continues eating. For the next twenty minutes, only the low hum of the refrigerator and outside sprinklers cutting on breaks the quiet. Obviously, she's given up on trying to drag me into a conversation and focuses on her food. Usually, relief floods me when people get the hint. And it does now. But underneath… underneath what feels suspiciously close to disappointment creeps, infiltrating and winding in and out between my ribs.

Ridiculous.

Switching time zones must be messing with my head.

Picking up my plate, I shove back from the table and stand.

"Thanks for dinner."

"Sure." She continues eating, her gaze on her plate. It isn't until I've dumped my plate in the rubbish bin and am almost at the kitchen door that she speaks up again. "Y'know, I've had a really shitty day. Like, shit squared. First, I assault a stranger with an egg. Then I have to face James and Jenna at the same time on my floor in front of my co-workers and pretend that I'm not imagining them enduring a face peel courtesy of Indiana Jones and the ark of the covenant. Then I find out that…"

Her voice snaps off like a dry twig, and I turn around, narrowing my eyes on her. But she's not looking at me; her gaze is zeroed in on the window behind the table.

"I find out that life isn't just unfair but a PMS-ing, bald-headed bitch. And then, we lose a sixteen-year-old boy who OD'd. So yes, shitty. All I want is to come home—or what's home for the next few days—pig out on comfort food, drink wine and be with someone who doesn't need something, looks at me with pity or is dying. Just maybe, a kind word. Just one." Suddenly, I'm on the receiving end of a glare that's golden fire. "You don't know me, and I don't know you. And I get you have this brooding artist thing going on. But we're stuck together for the near future, and would not being an asshole have killed you? Today of all days?"

She doesn't allow me time to reply. Not that I could've. Not when beneath the sparks in her whiskey eyes lurks shadows. I'm intimately familiar with those. Inside them conceal pain. Disappointment. Fear.

I turn more fully toward her, frowning. The "What's wrong?" crawls up my throat, hovers on my tongue. But before I can ask, she jackknifes from the table and stalks from the room.

All I can do is stare.

And never have I felt more like the arsehole she called me.

CHAPTER 4

AXEL

For the last half-hour, I've stared up at my ceiling, listening, unable to sleep. Could be because it's my second night in a strange house. Could be because my conscience—that irritating li'l fucker—is still bitching at me from earlier in the kitchen.

Or it could be *Bohemian Rhapsody* pouring through the walls of the garage into my apartment. The latest track in the personal Queen concert that my flatmate has been blasting at "take this, mate" volume for thirty minutes.

Not that Queen doesn't fucking rock. But at—I pick up my cell phone and tap the screen—one-seventeen in the morning, not so much.

When Bohemian Rhapsody slides into *Radio Gaga*, I throw back the sheet with a sigh. Snagging my sweatpants off the floor, I drag them up my legs and over my hips. I don't bother with a shirt or socks and cross the room to the door that leads to the garage. As soon as I step through, bright light assaults my eyes. Squinting, I take in the organized shelves, bins, tools and—*holy fuck.*

A Pontiac GTO.

I'm not a gear head, but I recognize this classic beauty with its black finish and legendary red interior. The sleek lines of the car are like the deadly curves of a woman. What I wouldn't give to hear its engine, that deep, smooth rumble… a panther's rumble. If it was a woman, she would be a pinup —bold, unashamedly proud of its body, and hot as fuck. It's every teen boy's—hell, grown man's—wet dream of a car.

And I'm drooling.

The bonnet is up, and I circle the rear, centimeters of air and space separating my worshipful fingers from the chrome side panels and passenger door. Yeah, I want to touch, to caress. But leaving my prints on this gorgeous paint crosses into the sacrilegious. I near the front of the car… and suck in a jagged breath that scrapes my throat. Just when I thought the vehicle couldn't get sexier, I glimpse the woman bent under the bonnet.

Lust barrels into me with wild, swinging fists. For a second, I close my eyes, attempting to block out the sight, but it's branded on my eyelids, my brain. And image of that petite but incredibly built body once more clothed in a thin tank top and tiny shorts that reveal far more than it covers. There's confidence in those slender shoulders, grace in the arch of her back, strength in the thickness of her thighs, and an incongruous vulnerability in her bare feet.

Together, she and the muscle car are a power couple, and all that black chrome and steel is an extension of her blatant sexuality.

Goddamn. I could come just staring at them.

Before I do something that could get my balls kicked to the back of my throat or arrested—possibly both—I edge around her and pick up the cell phone from off the shelf. Pressing the pause button on the screen, Freddie Mercury abruptly stops bemoaning the demise of the radio from the small, squat speaker.

"What the f— Ow!" Zenobia's head meeting the underside of the bonnet echoes in the small garage like a crack of thunder.

I wince. Fuck. That had to hurt.

"Son of a *bitch,*" she hisses, her hand flying to the offended area.

Before I can question the wisdom of my actions, I move forward and, gently removing her hand, cup the back of her head, rubbing my thumb over the sore spot. She stiffens, and I clench my jaw. I shouldn't be touching her—not without her permission. And not with her spicy, earthy scent drifting from her skin to my nose. She's hot, spiced cider and the fresh, dew-soaked earth on a misty morning. And underneath, subtler musky notes that I instinctively know are all *her.*

Yeah, touching her? A mistake. And yet, I don't drop my hand. I don't inject space between us. Instead, I carefully massage her scalp, and she doesn't shift away from me. That sends a hot bolt of sizzling satisfaction through me— and a staticky crackle of warning. I shouldn't care at all that she's not avoiding my touch, that she's accepting it. But the low rumble of almost primitive approval still resonates in my chest.

"Thank you," she murmurs, reaching up and covering my hand with hers.

Now it's my turn to imitate a statue. And close my eyes against the heat that licks over my body. I lock down the growl that threatens to roll out of me. *Calm down,* I silently bark down at my hardening cock. *It's a fucking hand, and it's nowhere near you.*

My cock doesn't give a damn. Stubborn and optimistic bastard.

Sliding my hand from under hers, I clear my throat and shuffle back a couple of steps. And quickly adjust my dick before she can glance down and get visual affirmation of how sweatpants do shit all to hide an erection.

Turning, she props a hip against the car, folding her arms over her chest. I deserve the Victoria Cross for not glancing down and checking out for myself what that does for her breasts. Amazing effects that even Peter Jackson couldn't rival, I bet.

"What're you doing up?"

I arch an eyebrow, then slide a meaningful glance at the now silent speaker. "I love Queen as much as the next person, but not bleeding through the walls at one in the morning."

She winced. "Sorry. I didn't even think about the music being so loud it could disturb you."

"No worries." I hike my chin toward the GTO. "What're you doing?"

I really wanted to ask how in the hell she'd ended up with a car like *that*? But in my head, even I could hear how sexist that might sound. Best not to piss her off... again.

She smiles, then turns back to the raised bonnet.

"Changing the oil in my girl," she practically purrs, smoothing her palm over the chrome. "Whenever I'm stressed or can't sleep, working on her always relaxes me." Glancing over her shoulder, she smirks. "You like her?"

I nod.

"She's an absolute beauty." She picks up a wrench, still stroking the like the car's a long-lost friend... or a lover. "1969 Pontiac GTO Hardtop. With a 400 cubic inch, 370 horsepower, Ram Air IV engine. She belonged to my grandfather, and we used to spend hours together on her. He taught me everything I know about cars. Taught me how to drive in her. Taught me how to outrace the cops in a street race in her."

She sighs, flipping the tool in her hand. "Good times."

I stare at her, mind blanking. A scene straight from *Fast & Furious* with an older man with her eyes and a younger version of Zenobia riding shotgun races through my head. Oh hell no. She's taking the fucking mick on that last one. Has to be.

"Grandpop caught hell from Mama for that one, but damn. It was worth it to see how she handles."

Nope, she wasn't kidding. Damn. I don't know whether to be horrified or impressed.

"I might've inherited my grandmother's temper, but my love of cars? All from him."

"What'd you get from your parents?" The question pops out of me, and I don't know from where. First, questions—or words, for that matter—don't just pop out of me. I usually have to force them out. And second, this need to know more about her—it's almost a compulsion. Chalk it up to never having food thrown at me or witnessing a half-naked woman maintaining a wet dream of a car.

Her smile tightens, strains, and the warmth in her eyes hardens just before she turns and gives me her back. "Bad taste in men," she drawls.

That statement's not only loaded but cocked with the safety off.

If I were smart, I'd dodge this baggage-shaped bullet and return to my bed to get some sleep now that the Queen concert is over. But my mother never accused me of being an intellectual giant.

"Tell me about your shitty day."

Somebody really needs to arse fuck me with a goddamn enema for this sudden case of verbal diarrhea.

She doesn't face me, setting the wrench down then bracing both hands on the vehicle. And I study the vulnerable nape of her neck, bared by the curls gathered in a large puff on top of her head. A few short, springy curls escape, and I nearly hum with the need to pinch one, rub it between my fingertips to test its texture. Find out for myself the ratio of soft to coarse. I visually caress the fragile but strong length of her spine, dancing over each dainty knob. Trace the blatant, unashamedly feminine curves of her hips down to the faint stretch marks on the backs of her knees.

Like one of the mythical beasts I often sculpt, I want to feast on that femininity and strength. Devour it.

Or let it bend me to her will.

"Now you feel like talking?" she scoffs. Picking up the wrench again, she scrutinizes it, and this is my punishment for being my usual, selectively mute self earlier at dinner. Zenobia shakes her head, then returns to changing the oil.

Several long moments pass, then, "To begin with, I started a one-sided food fight with a stranger who scared the hell outta me in my friend's kitchen."

I snort, but she continues.

"Then my ex-boyfriend of three years and the nurse he left me for decide to flaunt their brand-new love in my face. Which is bad enough, but then they both try to talk to me like we have anything to say to one another besides 'Bitch, please' and 'I hope you both contract a particularly virulent and stubborn STD from a bag of diseased dicks since I'm 98.66 percent sure you were fucking behind my back.'"

Well… damn.

"Then, I get a phone call that…" She abruptly breaks off whatever she's about to say, and a muscle ticks along her clenched jaw. "A call that didn't make my day any better. And then a six-year-old girl who was involved in a car accident coded. We brought her back, but she's in ICU after emergency surgery."

"Jesus," I breathe.

"Yeah. It's always the kids who hit you the hardest. She was so small, so fragile and helpless…" Her voice trails off like smoke, shoulders so tense they almost reach her ears. Giving her head a shake, she clears her throat. "Anyway, like I said, shitty."

I shift forward, the almost primal urge to protect, to shield, to somehow ease that pain saturating her voice. Pain she's trying so hard to conceal but can't. That wound inside her—whether from the hurt child or dumb-as-a-fucking-box-of-rocks ex—bleeds, and no flippant tone or nonchalant shrug can plug the hemorrhaging.

I'm helpless, staring down at my big hands that can shape and bend metal but not fix this for her.

"You wanna fuck?"

"*Shit!*" She jerks back, the wrench tumbling from her hand and clinking into the depths of the car. Cursing again, she retrieves it and whips around to face me. She blinks, her mouth dropping open the tiniest bit. Blinks again. "Say what now?"

"Do you wanna fuck?" I offer again.

And it *is* an offer, no matter how unwieldy and clumsy it came out. Sex always worked with my ex. If she was pissed, weepy or frustrated, riding my dick seemed to take her mind off of what was bugging her. Communication, my lack of ambition, my hermit-like tendencies—those had been issues in our relationship. Fucking? No. Hell, it'd been the only thing I could do right for her. My body, my cock... they'd been the only things of worth I'd possessed. The only things that'd seemed to bring her happiness, contentment. Before even they hadn't been enough.

And she hadn't been the only one. Sooner or later the few relationships I had ended because I couldn't be who they needed.

I part my lips, try to shovel out the explanation. To clarify so my proposition sounds less crude. But nothing emerges. As usual. The words lodge in my throat. Strangled by the abnormal fear that they won't be the right ones, that they'll cause more damage than good, that they won't be adequate.

Her lips finally snap closed, and humor flashes in her eyes.

"As a bit inappropriate and oddly... sweet as your

gesture is, I'm going to have to pass." She snickers. "Just out of curiosity though. Does that usually work for you?"

Laugh it off, you arse. The waspish and insistent voice rebounds against my skull, and the muscles in my shoulder tightens in preparation for the casual shrug. The teasing "Dunno. You tell me" crowds onto my tongue like a traffic jam, but once more, I fail the socially appropriate test. I remain mute.

And maybe that silence screams the truth. If a picture is worth a thousand words, then my silence is a goddamn soliloquy, because the humor in her gaze fades, replaced by something else. Something that seems a little too disturbingly similar to pity. And a quiet but simmering anger.

"You might not be much of a talker, but people—me, included—aren't too good at listening either. At seeing." Her soft tone hardens, shards of amber glinting in her eyes. For a moment, the full, sensuous curves of her mouth flatten into a grim line. "And whoever gave you the impression that all you have to offer is your dick—whatever bitch used you for it—ain't shit."

Now it's my turn to blink, to stare. At the vehemence in her voice. The fury. And not *at* me. *For* me.

"Same goes for your ex," I mutter.

Her eyebrows wing high. Whether at what I said or the fact I'm speaking at all, I don't know. But since I'm on a roll —for me, anyway—I keep going.

"If the bawbag couldn't hack being your man, then fuck him. His shit to deal with, not yours. Probably find a sterner spine on a worm with a fucked-up case of scoliosis."

"Bawbag? Fucked up case of..." She stares at me. Then

throws her head back and cackles, her throaty laughter bouncing off the walls of the garage, echoing until her hilarity fills the space.

The sound of it settles in my chest, burrowing deep, before sliding lower. Shit. Never got hard from laughter before. But then, I've never heard Zenobia's before.

"Oh my God," she wheezes, swiping the back of her hand over her eyes. "Damn, I love you Brits. Even you broody ones." She grins, and the beauty in it, the freedom of it, sends me mentally crab-walking back and away.

Like a vampire desperately trying to flee the gorgeous but lethal sun, I retreat both physically and emotionally. That smile, that penetrating warmth and loveliness... It's dangerous to a man who's used to being cloaked in the darkness, huddled in the frigid cold. They've become my shield, my protection. And she threatens to pierce them. To make me crave the heat of the light—of her light.

Even knowing she'll leave me exposed, defenseless. Fucking destroyed.

On the pretense of turning her music back up, I turn from her, granting myself a temporary reprieve. At least long enough to escape and regroup. Picking up her phone again, I wait for the screen to flash on, and then I press the play button. In the next second, Queen once again blares loud enough to drown out any conversation.

It's what I want. The perfect diversion and way to end this impromptu and misguided visit at whatever-the-fuck-in-the-morning. I can just walk out, return to my apartment, and stare at the ceiling. And I move in that direction, my feet following my brain's order.

Yet, the fuckers rebel. Halting right next to her. So close, my chest presses into her shoulder. Even as "what the bloody fuck?" ricochets off my skull, I bend my head over hers. My lips accidently graze the tip of her ear, but I don't shift away. Neither does she. And I don't miss the shiver that works its way through that petite, tight body.

"I would've let you use me, pet," I murmur.

Not waiting for her reply, I stride past her and don't stop until my door is closed and the mattress meets my back.

And my fist strangles my cock.

My cum splashes my stomach in thick, hot ropes to Under Pressure.

The fucking irony is not lost on me.

CHAPTER 5

would've let you use me, pet.

Nearly twenty-four hours later, and that grit and gravel voice still echoes in my head. That enigmatic and entirely too provocative statement has been tripping through my mind all day like the clumsiest of bitches. Not to mention, at odd points throughout the day, I could still feel the light brush of that too-full, stern mouth over my ear. Growling a curse, I rub the offending tip as I step out of the hospital into the evening air, hating that even now it tingles.

I pulled the mature thing this morning and avoided him. But I think he stole my idea, because the house had carried an empty feeling all day until I'd left for work. Which makes no sense when I think of it. I'd been alone in Gabrielle and Julian's house for a couple of days before Axel showed up, and their home had never felt *empty*. I'm no masochist, so I'm refusing to think on it. Fortunately, fevers, a couple of accidents, and a heart attack among other things had aided in that endeavor.

And if that doesn't sound eleventy shades of shitty, then I don't know what does. The misfortunes and poor health of others should not be a boon for my lack of concentration.

And yet, here we are.

Because without the hectic pace of the ER today, I would've drowned in the memory of the haunted—no, hunted—look in those blue eyes last night when I asked him if offering to fuck a woman's pain away actually worked. I'd been teasing and had fully expected him to either shrug or give me one of those dry, sarcastic, and utterly British comebacks that I've become quite familiar with since becoming friends with Julian.

But he'd remained silent. And those eyes. God, those eyes...

I'd been reminded of an animal caught mid-fight or flight, frozen. Almost threatened...

Sighing, I pinch the bridge of my nose. Axel Wright, with his brutally beautiful, Viking visage, gorgeous body, this-side-of-mountain-man-hermit-grumpy demeanor, and haunted eyes is a puzzle wrapped in an enigma and boxed up in a Rubik's Cube. And, at this moment, I just want a pizza loaded with every meat possible, a *Z Nation* binge on Netflix and an Axel-free zone. I don't think that's too much to—

"Zenobia."

—ask.

Well, damn.

I turn, even though I know that voice that reminds me

of classic rock—rough, raw yet melodic. Memorable. And it's here. At my job. Which means the man is *here*.

Given he's spent so much time in my mind today like a squatter refusing to be evicted, coming face-to-face with him shouldn't threaten to shuffle me back on my heels. But here I am, locking my knees, praying that I don't assplant it just from the sheer intensity in that ice-and-fire gaze. Why can't his shoulders stoop? Or why can't horns with deadly points thrust from his head? I smother a snort. With how my uterus is preparing to throw itself at him like a virgin sacrifice, I'd probably just stroke those horns and coo about how sharp and pointy they are.

Jesus. This is why I avoided him today.

"What're you doing here, Axel?" I ask, shocked my voice sounds even, unbothered. And that's a total lie.

I'm so *bothered*.

His face doesn't betray any irritation at my abrupt and yes, borderline rude question. That unwavering gaze just roams over my face, brushing over my forehead, grazing over my cheekbones, glancing down my nose, dipping to my mouth. It's almost clinical and...and sensual. How those two go together beats me, but they do. And if the beading of my nipples and quivering between my legs are any indication, it's hot.

"I wanted to see you."

So simple. Nothing else. It's as if this man uttering more than two sentences at one time is against his religious beliefs.

And yet my body tightens as if he uttered the filthiest of dirty talk.

Clearing my throat, I cross my arms over my chest and

shiver in the October night air. "How did you get here?" Gabrielle had mentioned Julian hiring a guy to drive Axel around Providence until he became acclimated to the city.

"Uber."

I nod. "Right." And because this seems to be my new habit, I clear my throat again. Damn, he has this effect on me. I don't like it. "So, what did you want to, uh, see me about?"

His lips part to undoubtedly deliver the most laconic reply since the Spartans, but another voice interjects. And *this* voice is unwelcome. I cringe at this voice.

"Zenobia." James appears in my peripheral vision with —of course—Jenna on his arm. "Is everything okay here?"

Gritting my teeth so hard I'll probably develop a case of lockjaw, I turn to my ex and his new girlfriend. "Fine, James."

As if he cares. I don't need his pseudo-concern, and the best thing he could do for me—like a belated parting gift— is keep it moving. I have to deal with him at work. I prefer not to do it during my free time as well.

But he's obviously not getting the telepathic memo to get lost, because he squints at Axel. Since I know James so well, I can practically read what is scrolling through his narrow little mind. He's seeing this tall, huge, bearded man with a blond mohawk and tattoos painted over taut, golden skin bared by the short sleeves of a dark gray T-shirt. His lack of outerwear and imperviousness to the night chill— while the rest of us are bundled in jackets—only adds to the intimidating I-don't-give-a-fuck attitude that Axel exudes like a horny, ring-tailed lemur.

Sue me. I watch a lot of Animal Planet.

Don't do it, James. I barely contain a snort as my ex exhibits some latent courage gene and shifts forward in front of Jenna and partly in between me and Axel.

Really?

Really?

God, what did I ever see in him? Part of me wants to cup Jenna gently by the hand and warn her, "Jenna, you in trouble, girl," in my best Whoopi voice. But then… nah. She chose to lie in this bed—my bed, mind you—so she can damn well smother in it.

"Do you know this… person?" James insists, and this time, I do not refrain from rolling my eyes.

For the love of… "James—"

"This him?" Axel rumbles. And for such a big guy, he moves fast. Because one moment, he was several feet away from me, and in the next, he's beside me and looming over James.

Oh shit.

"Axel," I murmur, curling my hand around his rock-hard bicep.

Jesus, does he have a furnace burning under his skin? He's kicking off so much heat, I could curl up against him like a milk-fed kitten and just purr.

"This him? The worm?" he repeats, his tone harder, his grit-and-gravel accent snapping the words in half like a frozen branch. Axel doesn't wait for my affirmation, but with the smallest of movements, crowds James even more. David and Goliath. Except in this retelling, David would be squashed under Goliath's size 14 shoe. "She's not yours anymore, mate. So, you don't have the right to ask her anything, yeah?"

They could probably hear James' nervous swallow all the way on the banks of the Moshassuck River.

"I don't know who you are," James says, and I mentally roll my eyes. He just can't help being haughty. Not even with an inked, scowling giant looming over him. Oh, the poor, sweet summer child. "But Zenobia will always be my concern and friend. Which gives me—"

"It gives you nowt," Axel growls. He legitimately growls, and the reverberation of it vibrates through my chest, over my breasts, down through my quivering stomach and in my clenching, wet sex. "Friends, much less partners, don't fuck other women behind their *friend's* back." A snarl curls one corner of his mouth, his disgust as clear as the screaming skull tattooed on his neck.

"I don't see how that's any of your business," James shoots back. But the tremble in his voice kind of robs him of his righteous indignation. As does the guilt swimming in his gaze. "That's between Zenobia and me."

"Wrong," Axel grunts. "She's my business, and there's nowt between you and her, mate. You don't get to dick people over, then expect their forgiveness when you haven't even had the balls or decency to ask for it. Until you're ready to do that and not be a right wanker about it, fuck off."

He ignores James' outraged gasp—yep, an honest-to-God gasp—and jerks his chin up at a silent and pale Jenna.

"Do better."

With that, he grabs my hand in his and tows me away from the entrance, leaving James and Jenna speechless. They're not the only ones.

I'm utterly floored.

And I'm sure I'm gaping like a fish with a hook snagged in its mouth. When was the last time someone had stood up for me like that? I'm sure it's happened before, but an instance doesn't pop in my mind. My mother was-old school—if someone bullied me and the teacher didn't handle it, I better had. Because if she had to come up to the school...

I mentally shudder. I'm sure my seventh-grade nemesis Teandra Hall, her parents, *and* the principal still suffered nightmares from my mother having to "come up off her job." So, yeah, I learned to fight my own battles, figuratively and literally.

But this... Half of me wants to yank my hand from his and educate him on how I'm perfectly capable of handling James, and one late night conversation hadn't given him permission to butt in like some knight in tatted armor. By no means am I anyone's damsel.

Yet the other half? Well, that half longs to take a running leap, jump, and wrap my arms and legs around him, so tight he could feel my heart through our clothes, skin, and bone. That half yearns to bury its face in his throat and whisper thank you. For having my back. For deeming me worthy enough to call James on his shit. For... caring.

I shake my head, silently sighing. I'm a mess. A heart-fluttering, butterflies at war in the belly mess.

"My car's over this way." I veer off to the left where my everyday vehicle, a bright blue Nissan Rogue, sits parked. "Thank you... for that," I whisper.

He doesn't reply, but his big, long fingers squeeze mine. It's enough of an answer.

Moments later, I press the unlock button on my key fob

and the flash of lights greet us. I pause near the rear bumper, half expecting him to demand the keys. Every man I've dated hated to ride in the passenger's seat. As if riding while a woman drove somehow sucked their manhood out through a straw.

But not Axel. He doesn't even pause but strides directly to the other side of the vehicle, pulls open the door and slides in. No cajoling. No argument. No grandstanding.

For a man who could be a walking campaign poster for a Viking marauder, he seems to possess little to no ego. It's shocking. It's disconcerting.

It's dangerous.

"Dinner."

I glance over at him, my keys hovering over the ignition. The streetlamp from outside casts half of his face in shadow, creating a mask of light and dark.

"What?"

"That's why I came down here," he explains in his brusque, almost clipped tone. "You bought dinner last night. I got it tonight."

"You didn't have to do that," I protest. "You *don't* have to—"

"Dinner."

We've known each other for a little over twenty-four hours and he uttered only one word, but it's enough to let me know he's not budging. Not only is he broody, he's apparently stubborn as hell.

"Fine," I grumble, jabbing the key into the ignition. "Dinner, it is, I guess."

If only I felt as irritated as I sound.

Things would be so much simpler.

———

"This is your workshop?"

Brilliant, I mutter to myself, staring at the small warehouse in East Providence in the Waterfront District off Interstate Route 195. One, I'm the one who had the impromptu and utterly unwise idea of him showing me his temporary workshop after we finished dinner at the pub over on Wayland Avenue. Evidently, fill my belly with some truly excellent banger and mash—who knew sausages and mashed potatoes together was a thing?—and my gums start to flap. So, after a brief, but very noticeable hesitation, at least to me it was noticeable, he drove the ten minutes over to Valley Street.

Two, I'm lying to myself about the banger and mash. Not about its deliciousness, but about its magical loquacious potency. The truth is, as we walked out of the pub, I hadn't wanted to return home just yet. No, Axel hadn't suddenly transformed into this talkative stranger who revealed all his likes, dislikes, secrets or his opinion on Brexit. I did the heavy-lifting conversation-wise and yet... Yet, even how stripped down earthy and raw he is, there's something so calming about his presence. Like a bottomless, refreshing pool of water with barely a ripple disturbing its seemingly placid surface. Seemingly, because I suspect a storm whips beneath. Axel Wright strikes me as the Times Square billboard for Still Waters Run Deep.

And something inside me hungers to dive into that pool.

To see how far I can go before my lungs scream for air. To discover if I'll be swept up in the current and left battered and bruised. Or to find out if maybe, just maybe, it will quench an unquenchable thirst and leave me floating, satisfied.

It should alarm me that none of these options alarm me.

"Yeah." He jerks his head in the direction of the squat brick building, and I follow him as he moves toward the gate that surrounds a parking lot and loading dock area. With a display of strength that leaves my mouth hanging open and, okay, fine, watering, he heaves up the metal sliding door with barely a flex and roll of his arm and back muscles. "Through here."

He steps inside and flicks on the lights. I would say it's a typical warehouse, but seeing how this is my first time inside one, I can't. Small windows march high along all four prefabricated walls. Several beams stretch from the floor to the ceiling, and a couple of thick, industrial looking fill the space. And ooh. Tools. I'm a nurse who can identify medical, life-saving machines that would probably appear like space-age technology to most people. Still, staring at the plethora of machinery mounted to the tables and set around the area, I'm fascinated and awed. And more than a little intimidated.

"What's this?" I ask, almost-but-not-quite touching a piece of equipment that looks like a huge amplifier with knobs, coils, clamps, and nozzles.

"A MIG welder," he rumbles, standing a couple of feet away from me, hands stuffed into the front pockets of his jeans. "I used it to melt and join pieces of metal together."

Realizing that's all the info that was forthcoming, I moved on to the next machinery, my curiosity in this side of

Axel not in the least bit dissuaded or appeased. On the contrary, being here has only fed it.

"And this?" I touch a metal disc resembling a weight plate that slides onto a dumbbell.

"Flap disc. For grinding, sanding, and blending."

For the next twenty minutes, I pepper him with questions, and he answers them in his abrupt manner. But there's no hint of impatience about him. And man, do I ask questions. Angle grinder, four-inch vice, Grizzly cutter, air compressor... So much goes into his art that my head is spinning, even with his minimal explanations. Still...damn. No wonder his body is jacked. The labor seems *intensive*. And hot. And dirty.

And fuck, there I go. In the next instant, my mind is barraged with images of that big, hard body doing all manner of hot, dirty things. With mine.

I would've let you use me, pet.

Dammit. I growl at myself as that seductive and taunting statement rumbles through my head again. *Stop it.*

I smother a sigh. And here I was doing so well.

"What are these for?" I squat down next to one of several buckets of random pieces of small...well, junk.

That's the only thing I can call it. They're things that would litter a junkyard. And I should know, since I'd tag along with my grandfather when he'd visit them to hunt down parts for the many cars he used to work on. Motorcycle chains, clutches, scraps of metal. I hate to call them garbage, but that's what they are. Unlike the tools Axel has schooled me on, I can't think of why he would have buckets of scrap stashed around.

I glance up at him when he remains quiet, dropping a rusty ball bearing back in the container. "Axel?"

"What do you see?" he asks instead of answering my question.

Frowning, I rise to my feet, dusting my hands on my scrubs. There's more here than a simple question. The weight of it tells me that, but for the life of me, I can't guess what it could possibly be. What importance could possibly be attached to a bucket full of spare parts?

I shrug a shoulder. "Old metal and pieces. Garbage..." I trail off, because I've missed the real question here—I've missed the whole point. "What do *you* see, Axel?"

Again, a long, heavy heartbeat of silence passes between us, and in that moment, I swear something like shock flashes in the icy depths of his blue eyes. Almost as if he's surprised that I've asked. That I want to know.

But that can't be right. How can anyone spend less than three minutes in this mercurial giant's presence and not want to dig beneath that beauty-wrapped-in-barbed-wire surface? Not hunger to discover his secrets, his brilliance, the chaotic and stunning core that creates the art I've seen online? Traversing the treacherous terrain, that dagger-sharp landscape to reach that particular holy land would be worth enduring those scratches, cuts and bruises.

"What do you see?" I push. Because I can. Because I'm me.

Because I have to.

"What you do," he says, and for a moment, I think that's it. That's all I'm going to get, and disappointment wraps around my chest like poison ivy, tight, prickly and itchy.

But then he hunkers down, those powerful thighs

threatening to split the worn denim over his legs. He picks up what appears to be some kind of gear, and he cradles it as if it was precious instead of a hunk of metal refuse flaked with oily residue.

"There are interesting and fantastic shapes in clutches, chains, and other mechanics, which makes for equally interesting and fantastic shapes in art," he murmurs. "But mostly, there's pleasure in using throw-away pieces most people wouldn't pay a fiver or tenner for. Those pieces that people see as having no value. Those pieces that are unloved. Abandoned. Rescuing rusty tools and bits of rubbish and giving them new life, granting them value again..." He rubs a thumb over one of the ridges in the gear, the caress—and yes, that's what it is—tender, before he places it back into the bucket. "Yeah, I love the idea of taking the broken, the disrespected, and making people love and admire them again in my art."

Stunned. I'm stunned.

Not only because those are the most words I've heard him speak at one time. But the words themselves. The *power* of them. Chills run through me, and I find myself battling the inane urge to weep. To fall to my knees and weep at this man's feet and beg him to just shut up when he *never fucking talks* in the first place.

Axel Wright.

I had a premonition about this man. About his lethalness toward me. But I was wrong. So wrong. He's not going to break me.

He's breaking me.

There's nothing I can do to stop it. And the most dangerous part? If I could, I can't swear on my grandmother's favorite Bible jammed full of past Sunday and Women's Day programs that I would.

The fatalistic realization is enough to unglue my feet, and though I've never been a big believer in the "he who fights and runs away may live to fight another day" philosophy, right now I'm edging back toward the door we entered.

Panic does that to a person. Turns them into a rank coward.

But then I pass by the table with clamps and vises attached to it, and for the first time notice the huge sheet of drawing paper spread out on top. I draw up short, my breath snagging in my throat.

"Holy shit," I rasp, my fingertips hovering over the pencil drawings. Like it's a revered relic of antiquity, I want to touch the paper but am afraid to. But not because of some red braided rope or a security guard that's on standby to drag me out if I do. It's because of reverence, respect, awe... Because it shouldn't be touched by mere human fingers that can taint it with not just our oils and dirt, but our cynicism and realism.

And yes, I'm completely aware of how mystical and *woo-woo* I sound. But I don't care.

Because it's true.

"You did this?" I whisper as if we're in a chapel with vaulted, stained-glass ceilings with depictions of God connecting with man instead of a warehouse in the industrial section of Providence. "You *drew* this?"

He stares down at the collage of characters and scenes that all emanate from the fantasy classic book and animated film *The Last Unicorn*. His fists are stuffed into the front pockets of his jeans, but I catch the slight flex of his fingers under the denim. To what? Drag me away from the table? Snatch the paper away and out of my sight? Part of me can't blame him. It's almost too personal to let another person glimpse.

Still, I don't look or step away. I can't.

The Red Bull. The castle. The forest with its animals. Schmendrick. Prince Lir and Lady Amalthea. The harpy. Molly Grue. King Haggard. And, of course, the Unicorn.

I'm transported back to Saturday afternoons during my childhood—sitting on my grandmother's plastic-covered couch, snacking on her coveted peanut brittle, and sipping on my grandpa's ginger ale, watching *The Last Unicorn*. Knowing that as soon as the haunting song hit the chorus, my mom would shut whatever textbook she happened to be studying for her master's degree in accounting and come sit next to me, dig into the pilfered candy, and watch the cartoon with me.

Every time.

Tears sting my eyes, and my fingers flutter to my throat where a hot, thick ball of emotion lodges.

"Zenobia?" Axel edges closer, and his clean cedar and fresh air scent teasing my nose, both provoking and comforting me with his presence.

It's a struggle—an out-and-out battle—but I drag my gaze from the drawing to him. And here I didn't think I could find anything to compete with his fierce, wild brand of beauty.

But Axel Wright has been proving me wrong since I met him a little over twenty-four hours ago.

"I take it back," I breathe. "Last night I said you weren't

much of a talker. I was wrong. You say a ton." I wave a hand over the drawings. Over the renderings of a rampaging bull, an elegant, lovely unicorn, a magical forest, a decrepit, crumbling castle. "Right here. And every word is beautiful. Magical."

Clearing my throat, I turn and head toward the exit. Again. Determined to make it this time before he can surprise me with something else. Before he can show me another side of himself that will have me throwing aside the rule I've lived my life by since I was sixteen, lying in a hospital bed and sobbing as I handed my newborn baby girl over to my adoption counselor.

Don't fuck up.

I've never been an eloquent soul. But the sentiment is as profound as if Maya Angelou had penned or articulated it herself. Fucking up doesn't just affect me, doesn't just spin my life on its head so it's unrecognizable—so *I'm* unrecognizable. It changes everyone who loves me, who's connected to me.

Getting pregnant and turning my baby over to strangers to raise her as their own didn't just transform me from reckless, selfish teen to cautious adult, but it changed my mother and grandparents from trustful protectors to watchful, suspicious wardens. I no longer peered at the world through rose-tinted, carefree Ray-Bans. I wore—still wear—jaded, crystal-fucking-clear contacts that judge the cause and effect ratio to determine if the consequences are worthy enough of the actions.

In other words, I don't do *impulsive*.

And Axel? He's the very definition of impulsive.

He's wild. Reckless.

Temporary.

Knowing this—judging the cause and effect ratio as incredibly imbalanced—I'm still so tempted to wheel around, run back to him, and *jump*.

Which is why I keep walking.

Maybe by the time he joins me in the car, I'll have figured out a way to ignore the fact that I can't walk away from myself.

CHAPTER 6

My phone buzzes against my thigh, and I ignore it, focused on finally getting started on the first piece for my show. I don't know about other artists—I've never asked them—but for me, there's this period of fear. Of doubt that attacks me. Makes me question if I can drag what's in my head, what I've drawn on paper, out of me to my hands, to steel, to metal.

Some people might call it stage fright. Some might call it freezing.

I call it getting Mum'd.

Fucked, ain't it?

But for those moments, I embody every disappointment, every crushing fear, every staggering grief and rage, and almost buckle under it. Almost walk away.

Then, I get my shit together and get to work.

Slowly at first. Always slowly. Like a snake, sloughing

off the negative emotion, the whispered words, the harsh sentiments.

Then gradual speed. Focus. Determination.

Right now, I haven't hit that spot where I'm lost in the work, in the piece yet. That won't come for a day or two yet. But, I'm close. I'm nearing it.

If not for. The. Fucking. Ringing.

"Shit," I growl. Straightening, I shut off the MIG welding gun, carefully set it down on the table, remove my helmet, and snatch off my gloves. For a couple of seconds, I stare down at what's shaping up to be a skeleton-like tower that will top the castle. A piece of motorcycle chain provides the illusion of rickety stairs that could be one care-less step away from crumbling—

"Dammit," I bark, digging into the pocket of my cargo pants and tugging the vibrating phone out. Without really sparing a glance at the screen, I press the green answer button and snap, "What?"

A pause, then a crisp and amused, "Well, cheers to you, too, mate."

I barely suppress another growl. Then, what the fuck am I holding it back for? He interrupted me. "What do you want, Julian? I'm working."

My brother's best friend laughs when most people would've been put off by my deliberate arseholishness. "Ah, Axel, you're always such a joy. I've missed you."

He teases, and yet his words strike as sure as a chipping hammer. Part of me believes—has always believed—that he only keeps in touch with me because of Blake. It's what Blake would've asked of him if he'd survived that lake long enough to give a last request. Because that's the kind of mate my brother was. Kind. Considerate. Loyal. Julian's the same; it's why Mum and Dad love him. He reminds them of Blake. Allows them to hold onto the last pieces of him. While I...

Well, fuck. I really am a fucking daisy today.

"Yeah, I get that a lot," I say, my leg jumping. Like a damn addict craving his next hit. Only I'm jonesing to get back to work. "Aren't you supposed to be on vacation? What're you calling me for?"

Julian sighs, and guilt shoves against my rib cage. Fuck, that was me trying to be more pleasant. "Just checking in on you, mate. I wanted to make sure you're settling in okay. That the warehouse is to your liking."

"Yeah, everything is fine. The house. The warehouse. Fine. That Nate fellow talks too damn much, though."

Julian chuckles, and relief flows through me. The band that I hadn't even realized had my chest in a vise grip loosened a fraction of an inch. I can be a dick—sometimes purposefully, but most times, people take my lack of communication and preference to be by myself that way. And it's that behavior that's driven them away. Only Julian has refused to leave. Permanently, anyway. He'll give me space, but he's never abandoned me. Even when I've given him plenty of reasons.

Which explains why I'm here in Rhode Island.

"I thought you'd enjoy him." Julian's laugh has an evil edge to it.

Bastard. He knew what he was about when he hired Nate to drive me about. I smirk.

"How is your health? Has your asthma been aggravated

since arriving? If you need me to arrange an appointment with a doctor while I'm away, I can do—"

"Jesus, you're as bad as Mum," I snarl, annoyed all over again. Dragging a hand through my hair, I clench the strands in my fist, tugging hard. "I'm not an invalid or an idiot. Or your patient. I got a doctor, Julian."

"Forgive me for being concerned about a friend," Julian replies, a distinct chill in his voice.

I want to apologize. But I want to rail more. Not at him. But at the part of me that makes him view me as weak. I've battled that perception all my life. I bend and manipulate fucking metal for a living, for Christ's sake. And still, I can't get people—my parents, Julian—to see me as anything other than Blake's younger, sicker, weaker brother.

Who am I kidding?

I just want to be *seen*.

Last night I said you weren't much of a talker. I was wrong. You say a ton. Right here. And every word is beautiful. Magical.

Zenobia sees me. I don't know how a woman who I've known less than two days sees what my parents, people I've known most of my life, and women I've slept with haven't.

That both unnerves me. Saddens me.

Sends lust roaring through me.

"Forgiven," I bite out, shaking my head, physically trying to rid it of Zenobia. The woman has taken up entirely too much real estate there lately. And I didn't come all the way across an ocean for a fuck or a fling.

My art. My career. The two things I have any control over in my life. They're owed every bit of focus I have. Especially since they saved me.

"Now, are you getting back to your vacation, or did you have something else to talk to me about?"

"Y'know, Axel…" A pause and another sigh, but Julian doesn't complete the sentence, and thank God. I don't want to hear it. "How're you and Zenobia getting along? Has she stabbed you with a needle yet?"

I snort. Because he's obviously joking but he has no idea how close he is to the truth. Grits—still sounds terribly nasty—aren't a needle, but she still threatened me with bodily harm.

"No, but the week is still young."

Julian chuckles, but then adds, "Go easy on her, yeah? She's had a rough go of it lately."

"I know, she told me."

A long, deafening pause. One where I want to pick up my welding torch and pound it against my big, thick fucking head. *Shit.* I can practically hear all the questions and admonitions pinging around in his head before they pour out of his mouth.

"She told you," he carefully enunciates, sounding ten times more posh. Like my mother.

"Yeah." I flatten my hand on the table, staring down at my scarred and nicked hand.

Another pause packed with accusatory silence. "You've known each other less than two days, and she told you her life story?" he drawls, and it carries a hint of bite.

That thing about someone's bark being worse than their bite? Yeah, that ain't me.

"No, arsehole, not her life story. Just the part about the cheating ex, shitstorm of a flat"—still have no idea what that really means—"and having to work with the ex and the woman he fucked around with," I growl. "Anything else?"

"I love you like a brother, Axel, and no offense, but it's kind of hard to imagine you as confessional type."

No, no offense taken there. Still, he's not wrong.

"Is there something going on there, Axel?" Julian continues in a low murmur. "I'm asking because it wouldn't be wise. Like you said, she's just coming out of a bad breakup, and you're only going to be around for a few months. I don't want either one of you to get hurt."

My temper, fed by frustration, irritation, and—if I was a man more in touch with his feelings who could admit it—yes, hurt, snaps. "But here's the thing, Julian. You're *not* my brother. He's dead. And I don't need another one. Or a guardian. I can control my actions, decisions, and dick just fine without your advice. So just back off, yeah? But to answer your question, there's nothing going on with your precious Zenobia," I lie. "Now I got work to get back to. Cheers."

I hang up before he can reply.

Because I was a bitch to my brother's best friend who hasn't done anything but try to be there for me. And the little boy in me resents him for that. For Julian, I'll never be more than a charity case, a survivor's guilty burden. It's enough that in my parents' eyes, I'm the booby prize. I'm so goddamn tired of being that with everyone else.

Stuffing the mobile back in my pants pocket, I jam back on my gloves and helmet, switch on the torch, and turn back to my piece. Soon, everything—Julian's call, memories of Blake, this grinding, inconvenient lust for Zenobia—is drowned out by the scent of sweat and iron inside my helmet. Even through the head gear, I can catch the smell of burning metal. Like brimstone, and I'm the devil, reigning over my own corner of hell. And I love it. There's nothing like it. The vent hoods above suck out the fumes, but by the end of the day, tiny shards of black and silver metal shavings will litter the floor and a thin layer of fine ash will coat everything, including me.

I'm home.

Here, I always find welcome, not censure.

Not rejection.

No conditions.

Hours later, I stretch my arms above my head, tired, back and arms aching, but a good ache. A good tired. The kinds that come from a hard and productive day's work. And as I scrutinize what I've created so far, I'm satisfied.

Fuck, such a weak word to describe the huge mass in my chest. That never goes away. Never gets old. That sense of awe, of fierce pride, and indescribable, nebulous joy that comes from pulling on that image in your head and somehow coaxing your hands into forming it. It seems almost... blasphemous, like you're somehow closer to understanding God when He created the universe. Yeah, if I ever tried to explain this to my parish priest, I'd be on my knees with so many Acts of Contrition, I'd be permanently crippled.

Still...

I trace the edges of the dilapidated, frail and lonely castle of a king. Immediately, Zenobia's face flickers across my mind, vivid and blinding in its intensity. I can pick out every emotion, every nuance in her expression last night as she stared at my drawings. They're branded into my brain, and if asked, yeah, I'd deny it. But here, in this warehouse where I'm alone with my art, I can admit that I dreamed about the awe, the reverence, the... the passion. The glimmer of tears.

Zenobia saw me.

I agonized over every choice of subject of artwork, of show. No matter how small—even if it fit in the palm of a child's hand—or how big—if it was intended for the lobby of an office building. A lot of artists use their work to commentate on the shite-fest of this world, but I don't; I create for me. Does that make me selfish and maybe even a little narcissistic? Possibly. Probably.

But it's the truth.

My specialty is fantastical and mythical creatures. Because I got lost in them. They represent the world I wished I could escape to after Blake's death. A world of magic, myth, steel, righteous war, and yeah, the fucking happily ever after. Everything my real life doesn't contain. But as long as I'm working, I can pretend it does.

And this show's theme had been one I'd wanted to do for a while now. *The Last Unicorn* had been one of my favorite books when I'd been a boy, and still is years later. While most people rooted for the unicorn and even the wizard, I identified with King Haggard. So struck by sadness and boredom that when he found something that made him happy, he went to any lengths to amass it, keep it. Lock it away. For King Haggard, his happy had been the unicorns. My unicorn is my art.

And when Zenobia had looked up from that table and stared at me, telling me with her lips and her eyes that she heard me, I'd felt visible for the first time in eighteen years.

It was humbling.

Intoxicating.

Hot as fuck.

And it's the last one that has me dreading returning back to Julian and Gabrielle's house. Because though I resented Julian for warning me away from Zenobia, it didn't negate that he was right. I'm only here for a few months until my show. And I'm a poor bet for anything resembling a relationship—just ask my ex. Zenobia, with her tough mouth, brazen manner, vulnerable underbelly, and doe eyes, doesn't need my particularly corrosive brand of bullshit in her life right now.

Or ever.

What would a successful, ball-breaking, big-hearted nurse want with a selectively mute, abrasive, socially inept sculptor?

I could offer her a good fuck, and then what?

An image of that small, taut body with its breasts perfectly created for my big hands, nipped-in waist, rounded hips, gorgeous arse, and thick, beautiful thighs sends heat racing straight to my dick. In seconds, I'm hard and throbbing.

Jesus, she's a drug.

No. A goddam virus that stays in the blood, resistant to any and all antibiotics.

Other treatments are available to me—staying away from the house, working, fucking other women. And yet, as Nate pounds on the warehouse door, I pack my shit up, eager to return to the source of my sickness.

I'm fucked.

And definitely not in the way my cock would prefer.

CHAPTER 7

AXEL

I pad barefoot into the empty kitchen. Nate dropped me off nearly an hour earlier, and after a shower and change of clothes, my growling stomach has finally driven me in search of food. My brain is on board the Give You and Zenobia Space campaign, but my gut is obviously in full on anarchist mode. It's demanding to be fed, damn my pride or self-preservation.

Just as I tug open the refrigerator door, footsteps echo behind me, and I squeeze my eyes shut. Julian and Gabrielle's house is big, but not *that* big. Avoiding Zenobia had been a fool's wish. Slowly, shutting the door, I turn, but standing behind me is not the gorgeous woman with the silken almond skin and dangerous curves that I just jerked one out to in the shower.

It's Trish.

Shock and grief pile-drive into me, and I lock my knees from stumbling backward. My fingers lock around the handle of the refrigerator so hard, so tight, I'm dimly surprised the damn thing doesn't rip right off the screws.

In some distant part of my head, I faintly remember Julian mentioning Trish relocating to the States. But I don't recall it being here in Rhode Island. If I had, I wouldn't be standing here in his kitchen, attempting to keep my arse from hitting the floor. And my heart from clawing its way out of my chest.

It's been nearly ten years, but she looks the same. Youthful, lovely, kind. The same long, light brown curls, toasted skin and slim body she had when she'd been Blake and Julian's best friend. The Three Musketeers, they'd been called. They'd been tight all the way to the end. All the way until the moment on that lake at her parents' vacation house in Scotland, when choppy waters had capsized their boat and Blake, without a life jacket, had gone under and wasn't found until three days later.

She and Julian had even been inseparable when they'd come to comfort me when Mum and Dad had been too gutted in their grief to do so.

I'd pushed her away, too. Only unlike Julian, she'd taken the hint and hadn't pushed back.

"Axel," she greets me, smiling, arms outstretched. I don't stop her as she enfolds me in an embrace. Even manage to move my stiff arms to hug her back. "Julian told me you were staying with him while you worked on your show. I'm so glad to see you. It's been a long time."

Sadness lurks in her eyes, and I step back from it and her hold. Both are too much at the moment.

"Yeah."

Her arms fall to her side. An awkward silence descends

between us, and though words jam into my chest and crowd into my throat, I can't shove them out. I don't know what to say to her. And even if I did, I don't know how to deal with the bombardment of memories. The suffocation of memories.

Back home in England, they weren't as difficult, as heavy as *alive*. Not with Julian and now Trish as living, breathing testaments to my brother. To who I am in connection to them. To who I'm *not* in connection to them…

"Hey, I thought you were getting the dip—oh, hey, Axel. I didn't know you were home." Zenobia barrels into the kitchen, and I think Trish and I both breathe sighs of relief.

She's a damn lifeline, even if the sight of her in a pair of short-as-fuck cut-off denim shorts with ragged hems and a tight, yellow T-shirt that's so thin I can glimpse the outline of a lace bra might just kill me.

She glances back and forth between me and Trish, a tiny frown marring her forehead. And because in the short time I've come to know her, she hasn't been one to mince words, she asks, "What's up? You two look like you just bumped into each other after a horrible one-night stand." Her eyebrow arches high. "And since I know you'd never cheat on Derrick, and you"—she shoots me a look—"were sitting in a pub with me last night, that can't be true. So, what gives?"

When Trish shrugs and parts her lips, Zenobia jabs a finger in her direction, her frown deepening.

"And don't even think about telling me 'nothing'. I stab people with needles for a living."

Shit. What was it with the needles?

Trish laughs and holds up her hands, palms out. "Fine.

God, I don't know why I hang around you and Gabrielle. Might be fear." She shakes her head, then crosses to the refrigerator, opens it and reappears seconds later with a small, white tub. "I know Axel from home. I was best friends with his brother, Blake."

"Oh."

Just that simple word, and yet it says everything. That and the softening of her eyes like sweet, melting chocolate.

She knows.

Zenobia knows about Blake. His death. And if the information is from Julian, then the dirty details of how it affected me.

Humiliation burns inside me, so hot, so consuming I'm shocked my skin isn't ashen. It's one thing for Julian and Trish to know that I'm broken, but for this strong, capable Amazon of a woman?

Fuck supper—

"Right," she drawls. "The accents should've been a dead giveaway. I mean, two Brits under a roof owned by another one? What're the odds?" She waves a hand in my direction, accompanying it with a head jerk. "C'mon, you. We're having a girls' night, but you're officially crashing it. Wine, pizza, and a *Grey's Anatomy* marathon."

Trish rolls her eyes. "Which, might I add, isn't the least bit indulgent."

"Well, when they make a hit series about hot, horny yoga instructors, I pinky swear we'll binge it. In the meantime, it's my night to pick, and *Grey's* it is."

Before I can tell her no and escape back to my flat, Zenobia crosses the short distance separating us and wraps her small hand around my bicep and hauls me toward the living room. For such a tiny package, she contains the force of a hurricane. I outweigh her by at least fifty pounds and stand a foot taller, but the shock of her touch rips through me, propelling me forward.

I'm a puppet, and she's pulling the strings.

Minutes later, I'm seated on one of the huge armchairs at the end of the couch, three slices of pizza piled with enough meat to clog every artery in my body, and watching residents compete for surgeries, have sex with co-workers, and generally fuck up.

And damn if it's not oddly addictive.

"Did George just get hit by a *fucking bus*?" I bark, shooting straight up in my chair, my hands gripping the arms for dear life. I gape at the screen. Horrified.

The hell? Did that just happen? Damn, not *George*.

"I know, right?" Zenobia shakes her head, then tilts her glass up for a big gulp of wine. "All's I have to say is, don't piss Shonda off because you will not just die, but die a horrific, humiliating, ACME-anvil-dropped-on-your-ass death."

"You knew this?" I demand. Snarl, really. Because, goddammit. She let me get attached. "You knew he was going to die and let me sit here and watch this?"

"Aw, sorry, Axel," Trish coos, but ruins it with a burp. Red stains her cheeks, but she giggles and follows it up by downing the last bit of wine in her glass.

Zenobia immediately reaches over and refills it almost to the rim.

"But at least we didn't let you watch Derek get hit by a truck. Now *that* was just traumatizing. I didn't watch *Grey's* for two seasons after he died." Trish shudders and, cupping both hands around the glass, sips in commiseration.

I. Fucking. Gasp. I might even have pressed a fist to my chest. Directly over my pounding heart. "Derek dies?" That's it. I'm out.

"I think you broke him, Trish." Zenobia snickers, and my brother's best friend reaches over—without spilling one drop of wine—and pats my knee.

"No worries, Axel," she says, obviously trying to console me. "Next time we'll watch *Sons of Anarchy*."

I blink. Because one, I have no idea what *Sons of Anarchy* is. And two, next time? They want me to join them for this girls' night again? The thought of it has warmth unfurling in my chest and stretching wide… and mentally scrambling away like a scalded cat.

"Yeah, 'cause nobody bites it in a show about a motorcycle gang."

Trish whips her head in Zenobia's direction. "It's a *motorcycle gang*. That's pretty much expected."

Before Zenobia can reply, a knock on the door echoes through the room. I shoot from the chair like my arse is on fire. "Got it," I mutter.

Leaving them to their continued argument, I cross the living room and enter the foyer. A peek out of the door's glass pane reveals a tall, slim man on the other side. It's late, and this guy's a stranger, and I'm not taking any chances with either Zenobia or Trish's safety.

"Zenobia."

She cuts off mid-debate and glances my way. When I jerk my chin up, she climbs off the couch and approaches me.

"You know him?"

She peers around me then grins. "That's Derrick. Trish's husband."

At the sound of her husband's name, Trish jumps up and bounds over to us like a wankered gazelle. Just as Zenobia opens the door, she leaps into Derrick's arms.

"Hello, darling," she purrs. "I've missed you."

"I see girls' night was a smashing success," Derrick says, his smile indulgent and accent posh.

"You need help getting her to the car?" I offer.

He switches his smile from his wife and glances at me, his gaze sharpening even as he extends the arm not wrapped around his wife. "Derrick. And you are?"

"Axel." I grasp the offered hand and shake it.

When I don't add more, Zenobia sighs and nudges me in the side with her elbow. "A hot as fuck Viking just opened the door to the house his wife just spent an evening in. You have to give him more than that," she grumbles, then turns to Derrick with an eye roll.

But I'm barely hearing anything else that comes out of her mouth. A lightning bolt of lust strikes me center mass, crackling through me, deafening me except for the roar that contains four words: hot as fuck Viking.

Is that how she sees me?

Behind my zipper, my cock stirs, hardening and lengthening until it's seconds away from punching through the damn front of the jeans. It's one thing to want this woman, to imagine being wedged so fucking far, deep and tight inside her that I can't breathe without feeling every quiver and ripple. But it's a whole 'nother thing to know that she looks at me and sees something besides a rude, socially clumsy giant.

Goddamn.

Why can't we rewind twenty seconds, and I could walk away as soon as she opens the door? Turn back time so I don't hear what those four irreversible, earth-shattering words.

Because now I'm so close to becoming that marauder of the North that she called me. I want to hunt her down, pillage, conquer. Stake my claim. Mark her body with my mouth, my fingers, my cock, just as I want to immortalize her with my metal, with fire.

I step back. From her cider and dewy earth scent. From the finger-curling temptation of those shamelessly feminine hips. From the beauty of those curls.

From her.

"Axel is a friend of Julian's from back home, Derrick," Zenobia explains. "He's staying with him and Gabrielle for a few months."

"He's Blake's brother, darling," Trish whispers, soft enough that her explanation barely reaches me, but loud enough that I catch the sadness saturating her slightly slurred speech.

Derrick hums a sound in his throat as he bends his head over his wife's and presses a kiss to her hair. Then he looks at me again, an understanding in his gaze that has my skin crawling, itching, needing to slap at it. Hiking up my chin at him, I whip around and escape.

Pausing next to the coffee table, I grab the empty pizza boxes and bottles of wine and head for the kitchen. The boxes don't deserve all the aggression I pour into ripping them apart, but ain't shit in life fair.

"Here. Let me get those bottles."

I don't stop decimating cardboard, but my muscles tighten in reaction to that husky voice. My gut clenches, and my cock... Well, that greedy, randy bastard stands at strict attention as if she were a lieutenant and it's enlisted in the British Army.

The kitchen is filled with the harmony of me ripping boxes and her washing wine bottles. Curiosity pokes at me. What is she saving them for—recycling? Rebottling? Making her own wine?

She finishes rinsing the glass out, wipes the bottles off with a paper towel, then sets them on the counter to dry. When she catches me looking at her, she narrows her eyes on me.

"I can see the wheels turning in that head of yours. And I also know you're trying really hard not to ask. But go ahead, Axel. Ask."

She's right. I've made a habit of not asking anyone questions, of not getting in their business—because they always seem to return the favor—that it's become second nature. Shoving the last of the cardboard in the rubbish bin, I inhale and face her.

And because it's her... because my fascination with her is a ravenous thing... because my inexplicable need to know more about her is only matched by insane hunger to be buried balls-deep inside her, I do the one thing I've never had the least bit desire to indulge in with anyone else.

I pry.

"What're you saving those for?"

A simple, rubbish question for someone else. For me? A huge step in a direction I have no business taking. Toward a woman I have no business thinking about, jacking off to, fucking craving.

"You're not the only one who rescues stuff people look at as junk." She smirks and spreads her arms wide.

Only Christ Himself would've been strong enough not to glance down as her breasts lifted under her tight T-shirt. And I'm nowhere near as sainted as Jesus. I'm that branch of the family He doesn't like to talk about. So, my gaze lingers on the soft-looking flesh rising above the V-neck. Traces the lacy pattern of her bra beneath the thin material. I jerk my focus away. But not before I catch the outline of her beaded nipples.

Fuck.

I flex my fingers, curling them into my palm, straightening them. Foreseeing another night of them strangling my dick.

"I'm a self-proclaimed DIY queen," she continues confessing. "I like to repurpose things. Like, those wine bottles might become dish soap dispensers, a mini-garden or tiki torches. YouTube videos are goldmines for ideas." She snorts. "I used to drive James crazy, just showing up from thrift store or yard sale shopping trips with bags and bags of things."

She tilts her head and studies me in that analytical way she has that makes me feel like I need sutures to stitch myself close after she's done with me.

"You wouldn't mind, though, would you, Axel?" she asks softly. "You'd probably dig through my haul and see what you could use."

She huffs out a laugh and shakes her head, turning away from me, not expecting an answer. Which is good. Because I'm not capable of giving one to her. Not when an image of us sitting together on the floor of my cottage, her cradled between my legs as we burrow through her shopping finds, blink and waver in my mind.

The mental picture rocks me.

Scares me.

Stirs me.

"I— Never mind." She laughs, and for the first time since I've known her—all forty-eight hours—it strikes me as nervous.

And it doesn't sit right.

Not on this warrior queen.

"What?" I demand, crossing my arms over my chest.

"I don't pretend to compare my hobbies to what you do for a living." She snatches another paper towel off the roll and proceeds to wipe down the counter. I don't know if the wine or the nerves has her cleaning as if I have a shiv directed at her back, but she's definitely going at it and avoiding looking at me. "Art is your passion, and I do this for fun. So, I'm not minimizing your process or projects in anyway—"

"Zenobia."

"Yeah?"

"Stop with the scrubbing."

Instead of bristling at my command, she exhales a heavy, loud breath, tosses the paper in the rubbish bin, and faces me.

"What are you trying to say?"

She wrinkles her nose and props a shapely hip against

the counter, her fingers curling around the edge. "Fine, give me a minute, okay?"

Since silence is what I do, I remain quiet, granting her all the time she needs.

"I love my job, but there's no room for creativity. It's high stakes, pressure, and the wrong decisions, mistakes, mean life and death consequences. So, when I want to unwind, to relax, it's with something that's the complete opposite of where I spend a good part of my life. Some people would call it using the other side of my brain. I call it using the other side of my soul. My spirit. I'm so dramatic," she scoffs.

Her self-deprecation is thick, and the order, "Don't do that," sits heavy on my tongue. Her feelings and her needs are valid, and she shouldn't depreciate them. Or allow anyone else to. Because something tells me that others have done exactly that. And it doesn't take Sherlock Holmes-level deduction skills to figure out who one of those "others" were. Fucking James again.

"For me, working on my projects is a solitary process, and I prefer it that way, because all day or night, I'm part of a team. But when I'm attempting to figure out how to make plant hangers out of old spoons, I can get lost in my head. I can experiment, try new things knowing that if I fuck up, the worst thing that could happen is I'll have to throw away a spoon and no one might be seriously injured. And then"—she shifts her weight, her hands twisting in front of her, her face and golden-brown eyes lighting up with a soft, delighted smile—"there's something so, so magical about birthing an idea from my mind into reality. It's like returning to that carefree time in kindergarten when your sole job was being creative and having fun. Y'know, before they killed it for us with good grades, popularity, ambition, and winning at any cost. But when I'm working on these projects, I'm that kindergartner again."

She lets out another of those self-effacing little laughs that I want to ban from ever escaping her lips. They should be a crime coming from her.

"I'm sorry. I didn't mean to say all of that. Must be the wine talking."

"Don't ever apologize to me."

She blinks, and I grind my teeth together. Hard.

This is why I don't talk. Too much. Sometimes I feel too fucking much, and the words come out intense, inappropriate. But I don't take it back. She shouldn't ever apologize for expressing how she's feeling. Not to me. Especially when it mirrors how I feel every time I weld, bend, buff, or polish metal. In a way, through my art, I return to the time before Blake died—I return to that carefree boy again.

I've said it before that Zenobia sees me.

But it's more. Zenobia *knows* me.

And goddammit, that terrifies me.

If I was smart, I'd turn tail and head for my flat. I'd close the door and hide behind it until morning when Nate showed up to aid me in my escape to the workshop. But the caution I usually exercise in my life has gone to take a piss as I approach her. Julian's warning takes a backseat to my need to inhale her warm, spiced cider and fresh earth scent directly from her silken skin. Common sense waves the white flag of surrender to my hunger to touch that petite yet strong body.

Every primal instinct engrafted on my DNA roars at me

to grasp the brazen curves of her hips. To dig my fingers into the flesh until the ridges of my prints brand the mahogany skin like tattoos. Ground my cock against her softly rounded belly and watch those light brown and gold eyes darken into amber flames. Watch those pretty, drag-a-person-to-confession lips part on a groan, a rough, needy whimper.

Burrow a hand into those gorgeous curls that remind me of restrained freedom and drag her head back. Catch that whimper with my mouth. Fall on it like the feral beast lust for her makes me.

Yeah, my every intention is to follow through on those urges. But as she tilts her head back and stares up at me, I abruptly pull up short. And instead of grabbing her and hauling her into my body, I enfold my fingers around hers, studying the differences of her smaller, more delicate but just as sturdy digits against mine. I'm humbled by the power in them. The dexterity, the talent. And now the creativity.

Closing my eyes, I lift them.

Brush my lips against them.

Her hushed gasp reaches my ears, and I tense, wait for her to stiffen. At the slightest hint of any resistance, I'll let her go. My intention isn't to invade her space or encroach where I'm not wanted. No, I want to... honor her. In the only way I know how.

With touch.

When she doesn't snatch her hands away or order me to stop, I exhale in—relief, gratefulness, resignation? All three, maybe. Lifting my lashes, I meet the astonishment in her eyes and graze my lips over all ten of the toughened pads and tips. And then the shorter, no-nonsense nails. Lastly, the uglier but still adorable knuckles.

Finally, I lower her hands. Step back. Step back again. And again. Until my next breath doesn't contain her scent.

But I can't escape the temptation of her eyes.

Or the quiet but simmering need that has replaced the surprise.

"Why?" she breathes. Stops. Slicks the tip of her tongue over her lips. "Why did you do that?"

I almost shrug, give her an abbreviated answer that won't betray how I've become more visible, more transparent with her in forty-eight hours than I've been with anyone in eighteen years.

Almost.

"Someone should tell you that you're beautiful."

Emotion flashes in her gaze, but I don't stick around to decipher its meaning. Retreating from her seems to be my go-to action. Belatedly, Julian's warning rises up out of the ashes of my conscience, and the caution I didn't heed moments ago blares like an emergency siren in my head, in my chest.

Zenobia's fresh out of a relationship with a man who betrayed and then left her for another woman. Despite the tough exterior, she possesses a vulnerable heart that doesn't deserve to be battered or toyed with again.

I won't be the man to do that to her. Because I'm not just a bad bet... I'm the worst. She's learning what I've already been well educated in over the years—letting anyone close means they will eventually leave. Whether by choice, or by death. Whether physically, mentally, or emotionally. Doesn't matter. Everyone leaves.

Since Blake's death, I've been chasing this ideal of perfection, trying to live up to who and what he was. And have always failed. Fuck strangulation or stabbing, death by comparison is the most painful way to die. Everyone loved Blake and people like him. People like Julian and Trish. Charming, gregarious, beautiful, and brilliant. Not lumbering, reclusive, chronically grumpy artists who prefer metal to people. Blake, my parents, Julian, my ex… None of them stuck. None of them stayed.

No. Being alone is better than constantly watching people walk away as if you're defective. Broken. Not good enough.

Me leaving Zenobia now—placing much-needed distance between us now—is preferable to her getting attached to a person who will eventually leave her.

And that's a thing I've become really good at.

CHAPTER 8

ZENOBIA

A couple of days later, I start another workday with Axel's voice and words echoing in my head. Is this going to be a thing? He says random, heartbreaking statements that send me mentally reeling, and I just have to deal with it? That doesn't seem fair. At. All.

Especially if it means I'll have to spend hours, freaking days trying to recover. Case in point, the night before last. Of course, in my twenty-eight years, someone has told me I'm beautiful. Even James has during our relationship. But no one—and I mean *no one*—has ever told me while basically worshipping my hands with their lips as if they were God-given gifts. Leaving me shaken, awed, and hot as fuck.

Thank God I didn't have to come in the day after girls' night with Trish. Because I'd been a mess, vacillating between avoiding Axel and convincing myself that a fling with a gorgeous, sexy, almost-stranger was a time-honored tradition.

Jesus. I shake my head, finishing up charting a patient's medical history and updating his record. I don't know if I'm going or coming with this man. Well… That isn't *exactly* true. Since that night in the garage when he offered to let me use him, I've been doing a lot of *coming*…

Why, yes, I have become a depraved, horny heffa.

"Hester. Dr. Lowry." Charge nurse Brenda Shannon strides over to the desk I'm sitting behind, a tablet in her hand. Immediately, I stand and round it, meeting her and Dr. Adam Lowry, the physician on call, on the other side. "Trauma room twelve. We have a rig coming in. Five minutes out. They're faxing over the demographics now, Hester."

I nod, waiting on her to deliver more instructions and information.

"Twelve-year-old female with trauma and obvious deformity to right lower arm following a fall at school. pulse, 100 bpm. Respiration, 18 bpm. Blood pressure, 135 over 85. Temperature, 98.7. She's alert. One of morphine on board for pain."

The facts running through my head, I move toward the fax machine to grab the sheet from the ambulance containing the patient's information. It would contain everything from the little girl's biographical data to her parents' contact info so we can call and request verbal permission to treat their child, to known allergies and anything else the parents included when they completed the school paperwork.

As soon as I stop in front of the machine, I grab several papers off the receiving tray, shuffling through until I spot the one I need. Dropping the other sheets, I head back to the desk, scanning the top. The fall occurred at a middle school about fifteen minutes from us. Accident during gym. Patient name Bethany Ma…vis.

I stumble then slam to a halt. Shock plows the air out of my lungs in a frigid blast that leaves deep, icy furrows. I'm too numb to bleed. Yet. But once the freeze thaws, I know, *I fucking know*, the bloodletting will be relentless, merciless.

Sooner than I want, than I can handle, the shock starts to melt and the pain creeps in, an insidious, gleeful intruder. The paper trembles in my grip, and I'm not sure, but I think the wounded animal sound that reaches my ears isn't from one of the bays in the ER. If I'm not mistaken, it's from me. From my throat, scraped raw from holding back a horrible, grief-stricken scream.

"Hester," Brenda snaps, and that no-nonsense voice prevents my headfirst, downward spiral into anguish. "Zenobia."

Long fingers circle my wrist in a hard grip.

"What's wrong?"

"I can't—" I rasp, then shake my head. *Get it together. You* have *to get it together*. Giving my head another abrupt shake, I scan the immediate area, but no one seems to have noticed my skirmish with a breakdown. I can't afford to do that here. No, I just can't to do that, *period*. I did that once. At sixteen. Not again. Especially not now. Not when…

"Zenobia, what's going on?" Brenda demands impatiently. "Do you have the demographics sheet? I need you in twelve after you make the call to the parents—"

"I'm sorry, I can't," I interrupt. When Brenda narrows her eyes, her face hardening in displeasure, I force my throat muscles to work so I can rip myself open and expose my deepest secrets to my supervisor. "I can't work on this patient. Because she's my daughter."

———

Hours later, I stare at the room where my biological daughter had lain, arm iced, pain meds administered after receiving permission from her parents, waiting for them to arrive. So they could offer her comfort. So she could cry on their shoulder. So they could ease her fear.

All the things I couldn't because I had surrendered all rights to do that twelve years ago when I'd given her up for adoption.

Unbidden, tears sting my eyes, and I blink them away, battle them back.

I don't have any rights to those either.

"What're you still doing here? You're not on shift." Brenda walks past me with her ever-present tablet, and her brusque tone helps me grasp onto the scraps of control I've been struggling to maintain all shift. She glances at me, and it might be my imagination, but there's a slight softening of her dark eyes. "Go home and get off my floor before I assume you being here means you want a double."

"How is she?" I murmur.

Brenda doesn't pretend to misunderstand my question. And in the same practical and straightforward manner that she took in my news about an until-then-unknown daughter, reassigned the room, and ruthlessly squelched any resultant whining from nurses and doctors due to the out-of-order rotation, she turned and faced me.

"We had the X-rays done and called in Dr. Taylor." I

nod, relief flowing through me, Dr. Rachel Taylor is one of the state's best pediatric ortho surgeons. The X-rays showed an open radial fracture with wrist displacement. Which, as you know, requires more than Dr. Lowry or our ER doctors are comfortable performing. A fracture? No problem. But something like this? No. We arranged for her to be admitted to PEDs, and Dr. Taylor performed a C-Arm setting of the fracture under fluoro. They didn't put her fully out for the procedure but administered Versed so she would be sleepy and Zofran for any nausea. They also had respiratory therapy there to monitor her. The procedure took about forty-five minutes, and she's now recovering in her own hospital room. If no complications arise, she should be released the day after tomorrow."

Okay, those tears? Eminent. Nothing I can do to hold them back now. To someone outside the medical field, all those technical details might not mean much or would be confusing jargon, but to me? They're everything. They tell me Bethany was given excellent care, that she's doing fine, and is on the mend. Brenda gave me a step-by-step walk-through of my daughter's care because I couldn't be there for her treatment.

Just another thing I couldn't be there for.

Stop it!

Giving Bethany up for adoption had been the best thing I could do for her. The best gift I could give her. Parents who could not only provide for her financially, but could offer her a stable home—a settled one without uncertainty and hardship. One a scared, unprepared sixteen-year-old couldn't.

Logically, I know this. But sometimes, especially now

when the guilt is like a hammer pounding at my heart, shattering it into so many pieces they resemble grains of sand, reason isn't winning.

"Thank you," I rasp. "For everything today."

She waves off my thanks. "Get out of here."

In spite of the emotional storm whipping me to shreds, I summon a smile and head for the exit. But as I clear the ER doors, I turn, my feet carrying me back toward the hospital before my mind catches up and agrees to the plan that's already in forward motion.

Moments later, I'm on the PEDs floor and, after a quick chat with the nurse on duty, I find out Danielle Mavis has run home for a change of clothes for herself and her daughter since she will be spending the night at the hospital. Grabbing an apple juice and graham crackers, I offer to take them in to Bethany. Since it's pretty busy, the nurse okays it.

My hearts floors it for my throat and lodges at the base of it. Breathing is a commodity that is above my pay grade as I near Bethany's room. Yes, I'm violating her parents' wishes. I'm breaking all manner of hospital rules. I have no legal or moral rights to be here.

And yet, my feet keep moving. And they don't stop until I stand before the closed door and my hand is curled around the handle. Inhaling a shuddering breath, I press the bar down and enter. Suddenly, the apple juice and graham crackers weigh down my arm like a fifty-pound dumbbell. My heart is just as heavy, and only by sheer will do I keep my arm by my side instead of press my free hand to my chest and massage the ache.

Unlike the bland, functional layout of the ER rooms

downstairs, the pediatrics rooms are designed with providing as much cheer for children as possible, given the circumstances. Murals are painted on the walls, brighter-colored blankets cover the beds, stuffed animals and a couple of other toys are stored under the mounted television. The medical equipment and its muted beeping can't hide what the room is or delude a child into forgetting where they are, but the hope is to offer them a little more comfort than the clinical rooms on the other floors do.

Again, logical brain absorbs all of this.

But that messy, emotional side of me? Doesn't give a damn. Every bit of me is focused on *her*.

And oh my God, she's beautiful.

The last time I saw her other than in photos was a day after I'd given birth to her... just before I'd given her to Gregory and Danielle. And though a box in my closet—well, now my suitcase—contained a picture from every birthday, a part of me still envisioned her as I'd seen her last. This tiny, vulnerable, wrinkled infant.

But no. There's nothing tiny about her. Even lying down, I can tell she inherited her father's height, not mine. As well as his pretty hazel eyes. But the oval shape of her eyes—my mother and grandmother's eyes—the nose, wide mouth and stubborn chin? All me. Fear flashes through me. What if she notices the similarities? What if she knows who I am and orders me out of her room?

What if I've royally fucked up by being so damn impatient and selfish?

Turn around. I should drop the juice and crackers off, and turn around now before it's too late—

"Hi," Bethany greets me with the friendliest smile and a

wave with the arm not encased in a cast. "You're not my nurse. But you have food and juice, so come in."

Oh God. Part of me wants to admonish her for being so open and trusting, and just inviting strangers into her room. Even if said strangers are wearing scrubs. The other half, though? That half desires to crumble to its knees at her sweet voice and weep.

But I do neither. Instead, I scrape together the remnants of my professionalism and wrap them around me like a tattered but still-serviceable coat.

"Hey, Bethany." I smile, praying it doesn't appear as unsteady as I feel. But the frantic prayers I'm sending up must be catching God on a really magnanimous day for sinners because my voice remains even, and she doesn't eye me with suspicion. Rounding her bed, I pull the tray over her lap and open the juice and crackers for her. "Here you go. These should help further settle your stomach if you're still feeling any nausea."

"Nope." She grins, the green in her eyes glimmering bright with her humor.

If not for me staring at the evidence of her recently broken right arm wrapped in a hot-pink cast, I might question it. She's in a remarkably good mood.

"I'm not sick anymore. But I'll still take the snacks," she announces, snagging the apple juice and sucking noisily from it. Then she nabs a graham cracker and pops it into her mouth. "No offense, but dinner sucked. And my mom won't bring me McDonald's. You'd think after a girl breaks her arm, it'd earn her some nuggets, right?" She rolls her eyes.

"Believe me, no offense taken. If you tell anyone, I'd

deny it 'til my last breath, but the suckage of this food is why I bring my lunch every day," I pseudo-whisper.

She giggles. "I promise not to tell… if some more graham crackers happen to find their way in here tonight."

I laugh. "You do know that's blackmail? Who knew that cute face hid a Babyface Finster?" I wince, belatedly realizing which generation I'm speaking to. "Never mind. You probably don't even know who I'm talking about."

Bethany slides me impressive side-eye. "Of course, I do. Bugs Bunny. I'm young, not stupid."

"My apologies," I murmur, smiling. "I'll make sure you get those crackers for utterly disrespecting your cartoon knowledge."

"Apology accepted."

We grin at one another, and I'm struck with a realization. It's been a long time since I've been this… happy. Content. At peace.

Whole.

Pressure builds and thickens in my chest, shoving against my rib cage, and once more, tears prick my eyes. Dammit. To conceal my reaction which will come across as creepy and weird to a twelve-year-old, I turn around on the pretense of filling her water glass. But my gaze snags on an open drawing tablet next to the water carafe.

Water forgotten, I stare at the pencil sketch of a woman, most of her face hidden by a floppy hat, kneeling in a garden. The picture engages all of my senses. Though no sun is included on the page, I swear its heat beams down on the woman as her hands dig in the earth. I can smell the loamy aroma of the dirt, the sweeter fragrance of the delicate flowers sitting next to her, waiting to be planted. The buzz and drone of insects reach my ears, and I just manage not to swat their annoying presence away. My tongue is dry, ready for water after a hard day's work outside that has stained my skin, gloves and clothes.

Inhaling deeply, I lift my head, tugging myself outside the pull of the drawing. It's been years—almost thirteen, to be exact—since I've seen Danielle Mavis. But I'd bet my favorite wrench that the woman captured on this sheet is her.

"You drew this?" I ask Bethany.

"Yep." She lifts her left hand, wriggling her fingers. "Thank goodness I didn't break my left arm. Not being able to draw for the next six to eight weeks would've been miserable."

"You're amazing," I murmur. "Truly. I'll freely admit, I don't know much about art, but anyone can look at this and tell you're talented."

"Thank you." Bethany grins at me. "Neither of my parents can draw. Like, they're not even a straight line." She snickers. "I've always wondered if I get it from my bio mom or dad. It'd be nice to know."

Your grandfather. He might've been a gearhead, but he had the heart and fingers of an artist. He could sketch out the parts of a car engine and build one like they were sculptures.

The words rebound against my skull as ham-size fingers wrap around my throat and squeeze. Tight. Strangling me. *Oh God. Please don't let me lose it. I need to keep it together. Let me keep it together.* I haven't prayed in so long. Maybe since I asked Him for help in making the decision in what to do— keep Bethany or give her up for adoption. But now I need

Him, and it doesn't escape me that, again, it has to do with my daughter.

An image of Axel wavers in front of my mind's eyes, and I grasp onto it like a drowning victim about to go under for the third and final time. My translucent fingers trace the dark brown furrow of his eyebrows, dance over his slashing cheekbones, caress the arrogant slope of his nose, brush the carnal, almost cruel curve of his mouth…

I suck in a breath. One more. And another. Center myself on that scowling, brutally beautiful visage with its laser-bright stare.

Is he God's answer? I don't know. But I send up a "thank you" all the same, and when I turn back to Bethany, I face her without any hint of the hole she's punched inside of me with her innocent remark.

I've always wondered if I get it from my bio mom or dad. It'd be nice to know.

She's wondered. About me.

Clearing my throat, I pick up the carafe and pour water into a glass although she still has juice left in her cup. Nothing wrong with her staying hydrated, and my fingers need something to do.

"I'm hopeless when it comes to anything artistic, too. But I have a friend who's fantastic." Well, *friend* was using a bit of creative license. "His name is Axel Wright, and he—"

Bethany gasps. "*The* Axel Wright?" She gapes at me. "The sculptor Axel Wright? You're friends with him? Shut. Up. You're lying."

Yeah, maybe about the *friends* part. "Nope, not lying. I take it you're a fan," I say, dryly.

"Are you kidding me?" She ignores the glass I set on the

tray and gawks at me as if I'm Moses and I just brought down two twin tablets. And that she might tackle me if I even think about taking back what I've said about Axel, broken arm and all. "He's one of my favorite artists. My mom bought me a book of his sculptures with his drawings he worked from. They're amazing. *He's* amazing!"

Eyes round with excitement, she turns and glances at her sketch.

"I hope to be as good as him one day. He's supposed to be having a show in New York next year. I've been trying to convince Mom and Dad to take me, but so far, no luck. But I figure I have four more months to wear them down."

Determination glitters in her narrowed hazel eyes, and her mouth firms into a straight line. In this instant, sympathy for Danielle and Gregory Mavis flashes through me. Something tells me when this girl sets her mind on something, woe to anything that stands between her and it.

Oh, I like that about her.

Speaking of Danielle… I glance down at my watch. The nurse didn't mention how long she'd been gone, but I can't risk running into her. "I should let you rest," I say, even though my heart constricts at the thought of leaving after only spending a few minutes with her in twelve years. "Other than graham crackers, can I get you anything else before I go? Are you in any pain?"

"No, I'm good." She smiles. "Thank you for being really nice. You know my name from my chart, I guess, but you didn't tell me your name, though."

"Right." Panic crawls through me, and the acrid taste of it sticks to my tongue like tar. If she mentions me to her mother, Danielle might guess right away who Bethany has been talking with. Or maybe not. Does she know I'm a nurse? Did Sabrina share that with her and Gregory? Swallowing down the fear that I've fucked up any future chance of being in this little girl's life, I force a smile. "You can call me Z. All my friends do."

She grins, and I smother a sigh of relief. Waving, I beat a quick exit, briefly stopping by the nurses' station to ask that they bring her another pack of crackers. I hold it together until I emerge from the hospital, cross the parking lot, and climb into my car. But when I crank up the car and Lifehouse's *Hanging by a Moment* fills the interior, I lose it. This song spoke to me when I was pregnant with Bethany and stayed on repeat. Another sign from God? I laugh, and the scalpel-sharp hysterical edge serrates the silence into ribbons just before I break.

The tears I've managed to hold back spill out in a hot torrent that scalds my skin and leaves me hollow and so fragile I'm afraid to drive. Scared that hitting one pothole will leave me shattered into jagged pieces on my seat.

Minutes, hours—hell, maybe days—pass while I pour out my pain, grief, and worry. By the time I pull out of the hospital parking lot and carefully make my way back to Gabrielle and Julian's house, I'm so empty, the night breeze could easily topple me over as I step out of my vehicle. The front walk and steps to the house from the driveway seem insurmountable, and after unlocking the front door and closing it behind me, I want nothing more than a hot shower and to ease into bed. And hope sleep isn't a miserable game of hide 'n' seek where I'm the loser.

That's my game plan.

But it isn't where I go.

One moment I'm standing in the foyer, and in the next, I'm through the kitchen, the garage and standing in front of Axel's door. And before my brain can demand a scathing *"What the ever-luvin' fuck?"* of myself, I'm knocking on it. It's after eight, and he could still be at his workshop. Or he could be home, minding his business like I should be doing right at this moment. If I had any manners, I'd respect his privacy, especially if he's been practicing avoidance like I have been. Yet, here I am. Not going away.

I lift my arm, prepared to rap on the door again when it swings open.

"Yeah?"

Fuck.

For a moment, every chain of weariness weighing me down disappears, dissolved by the heated and humid lust that blasts into me.

All. That. Skin.

It's like the first morning all over again. Golden, heavily inked skin stretched taut over roped muscles. Powerful shoulders and arms. A wide wall of a chest that tapers down into a ripped ladder of abs. Black sweatpants ride low on a lean pair of hips that, of course, are rocking the delicious V thing that only the truly fit possess. Thick thighs strain against faded cotton, and Jesus… I momentarily close my eyes, because no way in fucking hell is he wearing drawers.

All moisture in my mouth evaporates. Yes, goddammit, I'm staring.

But Axel is *hung.*

Like, dick swinging down his thigh, that thing belongs in the Dick Hall of Fame's Big Cock Wing, *hung.*

My belly trembles, and deep inside, where neither man nor vibrator has ventured for weeks, I quiver, clench. Hard. The emptiness that hollowed me out all the way home takes on a different quality—a sharper edge, an acute ache.

Need.

I recognize it on a purely logical level. But until this moment, it's been purely head knowledge. Because I've heard about this kind of overwhelming, skin-clawing, get-inside-me-or-I'll-lose-my-damn-mind hunger; I've read about it. But I've never experienced it. James for damn sure, never inspired it in me. Now, though? Now, staring at that eighth wonder of the known universe—screw the world—I'd do anything, sacrifice anything, to have it fill me, wedge itself inside me, brand me. Wreck me for anyone else.

"Hey. Zenobia."

Shit.

Squeezing my eyes shut, I ground my teeth together. *Shitshitshitshit.* Was I really just ogling his cock like a damn penis stalker? Like Cyrano penning love letters to a phallic Roxanne?

Worse.

Did he really just *catch* me being a penis stalking Cyrano?

Shit again.

"What's wrong?" He shifts forward, and before I can move, his big paw cups my chin, and gently, but too firmly for me to even think about avoiding him, lifts my head. "You've been crying."

"No, I—"

"Don't tell me no. I'm looking at you," he growls. "What happened?"

I sigh, encircling my fingers around his thick wrist. "Axel. It was… something at work. I don't really want to talk about it."

"Something at work," he repeats softly, his hand finally lowering from my face. But his blue eyes ice over, the skin pulling tight over his cheekbones as his lips pulls into an almost mean snarl that, damn him, doesn't do anything to detract from the beauty of that mouth. "James again."

"No." I shake my head. "God, no. I actually think he might be afraid to come within five feet of me after the other night." I huff out a chuckle, although it's short and lacks any amount of humor. I'm too tired, too drained to feel much of anything right now. And what little I can damn sure isn't going to be wasted on my ex. "I'm sorry to just drop by, but I have a…"

I blow out a breath.

This is stupid. I shouldn't be here asking this of him. I have no right. It's pushy at best, completely inappropriate at worst. I mean, I've known Axel, for what? A handful of days. Not to mention this could get both of us in trouble with the hospital.

Jesus.

What am I thinking?

I'm not. That's the problem. This is cra—

That hand cups my chin again, forces me to look at him. Stops me from spiraling. Centers me. On him. I suck in a breath, and it's pure him—the sharpness of cedar, the freshness of soap and water, the heated *essence* of him.

"You need something from me."

It's a statement, not a question, but it's still loaded.

Need? From him? Oh God, so much. Especially tonight when all I want is to forget my pain, to fill the emptiness.

My nipples bead beneath my scrubs top and bra, and I lock down a moan as a corresponding ache coils tight, tight and tighter low in my belly. As my clit pulses, a tiny heartbeat between my legs, liquid warmth dampens my folds. As if my pussy is readying itself for the possession of the cock that I just blatantly ogled. It's literally weeping for it, begging me to give in and ask for it. To take what he offered before.

To be fucked.

"Zenobia." His long fingers gently squeeze my jaw.

"I need a favor. And please don't feel like you have to say yes," I say, practically shoving the words out of my throat, needing to get them out there.

"Okay. What?"

"There's a little girl at the hospital," I begin. *My daughter. She's my daughter, Axel.*

Swallowing the whimper, I substitute the confession with once more wrapping my fingers around his wrist. And hold on.

"She came in with a broken arm today and needed surgery. I'm sorry." With my free hand, I pinch the bridge of my nose, grimacing. "I'll get to the point. She's an artist—I saw a drawing of hers and she's really good—and she's a huge fan of yours. While we were talking, she mentioned how she really wanted to see your show in February but didn't know if she would be able to make it. I thought it would be great if you could come to the..."

I trail off, but he cocks his head to the side, studying me with those piercing, arctic eyes.

"You want me to come to hospital and meet the girl."

"Yes." My heart thuds against my chest. He can't know how important this is to me. And I can't tell him. Can't share that besides giving Bethany to parents that could offer her the home, the stability, the *life* I couldn't at sixteen, this is the first thing I get to do for my daughter. And I don't want to fail.

"What time?"

I blink. Blink again. "You'll do it?" I whisper, disbelieving.

It can't be this easy… can it? James would've made me submit a three-page, single spaced, 12-font Times New Roman essay with one-inch margins on the cost effectiveness of this request and any decision he made. And then he probably would've still said no because of the potential threat to his job.

"Yeah." He drops his hand, and only the last few scraps of common sense prevent me from grabbing for it and pressing that big palm between my breasts. Over my heart. "What time?"

Quickly, I run options through my head. "How about eleven? Do you think your ride can get you there? Or an Uber? I can pay—"

"I got it. I'll see you at eleven."

"Okay." Relief gushes through me, and for a second, I fear my knees are going to give out right there in front of him. "Okay," I repeat. "If you'll give me your phone, I'll add my number, and you can call me when you're close so I can come out and meet you."

He turns away, and yeah, dammit, I look. No, I fucking *stare* at that perfect ass in faded black cotton fleece and the

muscular thighs that test the limits of that material. He's…
art. Like one of his metal sculptures, he's steel and power,
sharp edges and fluid motion, a thousand stories
enshrouded in mystery.

He's beautiful.

"Here." He's back in front of me, thrusting his cell
toward me.

I quickly pull up his address book app and add my
contact info, then return the phone to him.

"Thank you for this, Axel." Crossing my arms over my
chest because the traitorous, so damn needy things want to
wrap themselves around his wide torso and back, I retreat a
step. "I really appreciate it."

"Yeah."

"Well"—another step—"good night." Another step. "I'll
see you tomorrow."

Before he can reply—before I can do anything foolish
like convince myself to touch him, ask him if I can just fall
asleep cuddled next to him so I won't be alone tonight—I
turn and basically flee across the garage, through the
kitchen entrance, and into the house. Shutting the door
firmly behind me and on temptation.

Who am I kidding?

There's no "basically" about it.

I fled like the coward I am.

CHAPTER 9

She's nervous.

I can't put my finger on what tips me off to it. But as Zenobia leads me off the hospital elevator onto a floor with pastel walls and all kinds of animals and flowers painted on them, I can definitely tell something has her skittish. Maybe it's that she hasn't stopped rambling on since she met me at the emergency room entrance. Or that she keeps tugging on the hem of her light blue top. Or that she hasn't really looked at me.

And I've noticed the latter, because I can't stop looking at her.

With her dense curls pulled up in a bun, her lovely, clean profile is exposed to my greedy stare. And I gorge on it.

Just like that golden-brown gaze feasted on me last night.

Did she think I wouldn't notice? As if I wouldn't feel the

almost physical touch of her eyes on my chest, my hips, my thighs—my dick. Jesus, how I managed not to harden and rise right then with her eye-fucking me was a minor miracle. But goddamn, it was close. Hunger had darkened those gorgeous eyes. Hunger *for me*. And when I asked her what she needed from me, I'd prayed she'd ease this voracious craving we both suffered and demand my cock. Demand me, plowing so deep, so hard inside of her that the walls would rattle with it like restless ghosts.

But she didn't.

And I wasn't surprised. Because God wouldn't answer a supplication about fucking anyway.

He wouldn't answer any prayers from me at all.

But then again, maybe I'm wrong on that. Maybe He did answer by saving me from assured damnation if I'd tasted that beautiful, lush skin and the undoubtedly even softer, sweeter flesh between her thick thighs.

Moments after stopping by the nurses' station where Zenobia speaks with her coworker, I stand next to her in front of a partially closed room door.

"Ready?" she asks with another pull on her top and a quick swipe of her tongue across her full lips.

The sight of that has lust grinding my stomach to dust, but my attention focuses on the meaning behind that gesture. "Are you?" I shoot back.

Her head snaps up, and she frowns. "What do you mean? Of course, I am."

Instead of answering, I jerk my chin toward the door. Exhaling a deep breath, she raps on the wood then enters the room, me on her heels. It's more of the same child-friendly decoration in here, a mounted television with that irritating-as-hell yellow sponge yapping away, medical equipment, and a bed with a young girl wearing a pink cast on her arm reclining in the middle of it. Zenobia greets the girl, and a smile blooms across her face, and shock jackhammers the breath out of my lungs. The eye color is different, but the shape of those eyes, the nose, the features and *that smile*…

Zenobia's taking the fucking mick. Last night she made it seem like this girl was just a patient, but it's obvious she belongs to Zenobia in some way. A sister, a daughter. They're definitely family. Why the hell did she omit that piece of information from the story?

At least now I get the reason behind her nerves. Anger and maybe the dregs of humiliation kindle low in my gut. Did she really think I wouldn't notice? That I was too thick in the head to notice?

"Oh my God, it's *you*! Axel Wright! Z, you weren't lying! He *is* your friend!" the little girl squeals, her pretty hazel eyes as wide as her grin.

Friends, are we? I slant Zenobia a look and barely contain my snort. I've never wanted to fuck my friends into next week, but sure. Friends.

"Well, you already know him." Zenobia laughs softly. "Axel, this is the artist I was telling you about. I'd like you to meet Bethany Mavis. She's a huge fan." Zenobia glances back at me, and her big, honey-brown eyes undo me.

Goddammit. Locking my jaw, I shove down the dark, gathering storm in my chest and shift my gaze back to the beaming girl.

"Bethany, when I told Axel about you, he was happy to drop by and see you."

"Really?" Bethany asks, and then, in a gesture that's so Zenobia it reaches inside me and fists my heart, she scrunches up her face in an adorable moue and shakes her head. "Duh, yes, really. You're here, right? I'm sorry. I just can't believe *you're here!*"

I nod at her. "Cheers, Bethany."

If possible, her smile widens even more, and her eyes almost disappear under the weight of it. "Cheers, Axel."

She shifts, and discomfort flashes over her face. Zenobia quickly moves closer to her side, and with a hand on her back, helps her adjust in the bed so she's sitting straighter.

"Thanks, Z," she says, then shifts her focus back to me. "My parents took me on a trip to England when I was ten, and we visited friends of theirs in Leeds. We went to a showing at the Sunny Bank Mills Art Space, and your sculptures were there. The ones from *Twenty Thousand Leagues Under the Sea.* Art was my favorite class in school until then, but after that, I wanted to be a sculptor like you."

"Thanks for that."

Yeah, I've received praise for my work before. But her unadulterated, innocent admiration warms me in a way none of the art critics' most effusive accolades have. It's honest, and the joy in her voice, her face… It's a joy at not just meeting me, but over discovering her passion.

That releases the usual lock on my vocal cords, and I shift closer to the bed, slipping my crossbody bag over my head and setting it on the end of the mattress. "Zenobia mentioned you draw. That's where I started too. Sculpting came later. If you don't mind sharing, can I see your work?"

"If I don't—" she whispers. "Are you serious?"

Not waiting for me reply, she picks up the medium-sized tablet next to her hip, but at the last moment, her fingers tighten around it. Her teeth sink into her bottom lip, and she drops her gaze to her blanket-covered legs.

"I'm sure they're not as good as yours…"

"Bethany." I wait until she lifts her eyes to mine again. "Everyone starts somewhere, yeah? You should've seen mine when I first started drawing. Forget it, I'd rather you not see them," I grumble, and I fight a smile as the little girl snickers. "Point is, I'm not here to judge but to meet a fellow artist. Besides, Zenobia raved about how good you are. She might be stubborn, can't carry a tune in a rubbish bin, a Swiftie—"

"I'm also standing right here," Zenobia mutters. "And I'm *not* a Swiftie."

"But she's not a liar," I continue. "She says you're good, you're good."

I wait, not pressuring her because I get it. Letting someone see your art is like revealing a piece of your soul. And inviting criticism of it. Sometimes I think we're a masochistic lot. Afraid of rejection, yet always opening ourselves up to it. Claiming we don't need validation, but our success depends on it. We're walking, breathing contradictions.

Or crazy as fuck.

After another couple of moments, Bethany extends her arm, offering me the drawing tablet. Carefully, I accept it, treating the pad like the treasure it is. As soon as I flip the cover back and study the first sketch—a man sitting at a desk, his head bent over a book, his glasses sliding halfway down his nose—her talent damn near barrels off the page.

No, that's not right. It pirouettes. Graceful, beautiful, dazzling, and yet, strong. It's a little rough and she has a lot to learn as far as technique, but Jesus Christ. She's leaps and bounds beyond me at her age. Anyone looking at this drawing couldn't deny her gifting. Because that's the only explanation for how a young girl could capture the nuances of this man's intense expression, the almost kinetic energy in his pose as he prepares to turn a page. I don't know for sure, but I bet he bounces his leg as he reads. That's what I pull from this drawing.

I don't speak as I flip through the rest of the tablet. Page after page of sketches. There are people, objects, even mythical creatures like I sculpt. It seems as if she's finding herself. I can already tell her—she's meant to draw people. Depict and celebrate their differences, lives, honesty, struggles—their beauty.

When I finally close the pad and lift my head, both Bethany and Zenobia study me with expectant gazes.

"You're fucking brilliant, Bethany." I should wince over my language. At least apologize. But I can't. I won't. Because sometimes you need a good four-letter word to get the point across. And she needs to understand how damn grand she is. By the light that brightens her face, I don't think she minds. And though Zenobia narrows her eyes on me, the corner of her mouth twitches. So, I don't think she does either.

"You're not just saying that?" Bethany breathes.

"Axel might be broody, a bit grumpy, and not much of a talker," Zenobia murmurs, her gaze fixed on me, "but he's not a liar."

I can't look away from her as she turns my words back

on me. Damn my heart for pounding at my rib cage like an anvil striking steel. Damn my lungs for constricting so tight, the air can't move through them. Damn my cock for stirring to life at not a teasing touch or a rough pump, but a whispered compliment from this woman.

And damn me for craving more of that admiring glimmer in her honey eyes.

Fucking look away, mate. Fucking look away and don't fall into that trap. I obey that low voice of caution in my head and focus on opening my bag as if it contains all the secrets of Stonehenge and the Holy Grail in its depths. Not chancing a glance in Zenobia's direction again, I remove my own pad, round the bed, and drag the visitor's chair close. Lowering into it, I hand her tablet back to her.

"Let me show you some things that'll help with proportion and shading."

For the next twenty minutes, I work with her, losing myself in the pleasure of art and collaborating with another person who loves it as much as I do. She's attentive, quick to pick up suggestions, not taking offense when I correct her, but eager to learn. By the time I stand, carefully rip out the sketch of Lady Amalthea from *The Last Unicorn,* and hand it to her, she has her own beautiful drawing of a fairy sitting on a flower, reading.

"I can have it?" she asks, gently, reverently laying it on the top of her pad. "Are you sure?"

"Yeah. Consider it a preview to the new show in February. You and your parents have reserved tickets for whenever you want to use them. I'll give the gallery your name."

She looses another squeal, reminding me of her age, and

I'm hard pressed not to grin at the sound that'd surely have nearby dogs howling in distress. "Axel, you're the best! I can't believe it! Wait until I tell Mom!" She does a wiggle dance that involves hips and her one good arm. "Thank you so much for coming by! And thank you for bringing him here, Z!"

Zenobia smiles at her. "No problem. Take care of yourself, okay? If we see you back here, I want it to be as the resident artist for other kids, not as a patient."

Bethany grins. "I like that. Okay, promise. You'll come and say bye before I'm discharged?" she asks.

Something flickers in Zenobia's eyes, and unease creeps back inside me, slithering through my veins, polluting the peace of the last half-hour.

"I'll try." Her arm twitches, fingers curling into her palm. My gaze flicks to Bethany, but the girl doesn't notice. Just me. Who doesn't miss a damn thing about Zenobia. "We need to get going. See you later."

"Bye!" Bethany waves with her good hand, and I still see her huge smile as Zenobia closes the door behind us.

"Thanks, Axel," Zenobia breathes. "I really appreciate—"

"Save it," I grind out, wrapping my fingers around her upper arm.

Quickly scanning the hall, I spot a room with Employees Only on it. I grab the handle, push down on it and enter. A couch occupies one wall, and a bunk bed with rumpled covers sits against the other. Otherwise, it's empty. Good, because if it hadn't been, this would've been a real awkward conversation since I wouldn't have given a fuck about an audience.

"Axel, what the hell?" she snaps, wrenching her arm out of my grip and glaring up at me.

"No, pet," I growl, advancing on her, then slamming to a halt. One, because using my size as intimidation is beneath me. And two, getting any closer to her where I can catch her scent, see the leap of her pulse at the base of her throat, is just fucking foolish. "You don't get to be mad here. Not when you let me walk into that room without telling me who I was seeing."

She recoils, her chin popping back as if my accusation is a physical blow. "I don't know what you're talking about."

I sneer at the weak pathetic attempt to dissuade me from the truth. "I just told that little girl that you don't lie. Now you're making one out of me."

Her sigh is heavy, but serrated. She squeezes her eyes shut, pinching the bridge of her nose, before meeting my gaze. "I didn't lie," she whispers. "I just didn't give you all the information."

"Quite same."

"Axel..." She stares up at me, those plush lips parted, but nothing comes out. She tries again. "I..."

Her voice might have given up on her, but those golden eyes? They haven't shut up. And they're begging me to leave this alone. To let this go. To let *her* go.

No way in hell.

"Start with why you didn't tell me I was going to see your sister. Or daughter? Which is it? Don't bother trying to deny that young'n isn't related to you."

"Back up," she rasps...pleads. "Please. Give me..."

I automatically comply, and she bends over, her hands

dropping to her knees. Her sharply indrawn breaths echo in the small room like ricocheting bullets.

"Easy, pet," I murmur, concern capsizing any annoyance at her deception. Cupping the back of her neck, I bow over her. "Breathe in. Slowly. Hold it. Now release it. Slow, pet. Slow. There you go," I praise as her breathing starts to even out.

After a few moments, she straightens, her back pressed to the wall, palms flattened next to her thighs. Eyes closed and mouth compressed into a grim line, it's the most... broken I've seen Zenobia, and I don't fucking like it. Not one bit.

She asked for space; I should keep backpedaling until I put the whole damn room between us. But something almost feral howls inside of me that she needs *me*, not more distance. Not to be alone. And though I, more than anyone, understands the desire for personal space—craves to be left alone—I stalk toward her. Not stopping until my arms cage her in, my hands and forearms bracketing her head. My body braced over hers, not touching but sheltering hers, offering whatever strength she requires. I won't tell anyone if she needs to borrow mine right now. As soon as we walk back out that door, she can be the indomitable Zenobia Hester again. But here, in this small room with the bunk beds and a laughably small couch, she can take from me and I won't tell a soul.

She tips her head back, and I can taste her breath. It's sweetness. And sex. It's light. And every dark, twisted thing my mind and cock could ever do to this mouth, this body. This soul.

Back away, my conscience roars.

This isn't wise, the Julian in my head urges.

I ignore both of them and don't move. Drinking her in like a man diving into a freshwater pool after suffering a hundred-year drought.

"She's my daughter," she whispers, voice cracking on "daughter." She swallows, and in appreciation of giving me this obviously difficult truth, I want to trace my lips up her throat, drop a hard kiss on each corner of her mouth. She closes her eyes. "I had her—"

"Open your eyes and look at me," I order.

She does, and the quick compliance is like a fist pumping down my cock—and a mule's kick to my chest.

"You have nowt to be ashamed of, pet. So, don't drop your eyes when you give me this. Look at me."

"I had her when I was sixteen," she begins again, that golden gaze staring into mine. "I thought I was in love, that my boyfriend and I would stay together forever. But as soon as he found out I was pregnant, he bailed. And I wasn't ready to be a parent."

Her voice hitches, and as close intimate friends as I am with guilt, I recognize it. Cupping her cheek, I stroke my thumb over the elegant arch of her cheekbone, silently encouraging her to continue. To purge herself of a story, I suspect she's never shared with anyone else.

"I had my mother and my grandparents, but it didn't seem fair to expect them to raise me and a baby. And they..." She falters. But then fingers clutch the waistband of my jeans and curl into it, hanging on. "They wanted me to give the baby up for adoption. I can't blame them for not wanting the added responsibility, and I-I'd disappointed them. But even then, I would've kept the baby if I believed I could. But," she shook her head, "I couldn't. I mean, I didn't have a job. I depended on my mother. And all my dreams of finishing high school and going to college—maybe those wouldn't have been off the table, but they would've definitely been so much harder. And financially? I couldn't do it. And my baby deserved more than I could give her as a teen mother. She deserved every advantage, every opportunity, every head start. And so, I decided to give her up to a family who could provide that for her."

She inhales, her grip on me tightening, drawing me closer, although I don't think she's aware of it. But conscious or not, I surrender to her need of me, pressing closer until only negligible inches of air separates our bodies.

"When she was born, and I saw her face, I almost changed my mind. For a moment, I couldn't do it. I loved her so much, the thought of turning her over..." A whimper breaks free of her throat, but she quickly corals it. "But that same love made me go through with it. I wanted the world for her, and I knew Gregory and Danielle Mavis could give it to her. With the help of my adoption counselor, I'd hand-picked them, and I was gifting my daughter with adoring parents who would provide not just a loving home, but she'd never have to worry about where her next meal was coming from. Or if the power bill would be paid. Or if she could join a ballet class. She'd have not just her necessities met but her wants too. I *needed* her to have that life. It's the only way I was able to give her away in that hospital room."

"You did good, Zenobia," I tell her, and for once, the words come easy. "It would've been easier to keep her, maybe even more selfish to keep her. But you put your daughter first."

Dropping my hand to her chin, I tilt her head up so she has no choice but to keep her eyes on me. To see the truth in me.

"There's no guilt in that. No shame."

For a second, her face crumbles, but only for a second. She draws in a breath and closes her eyes. But then, as if remembering my demand, her lashes lift.

"I shouldn't have approached her when she came in yesterday," she confesses hoarsely. "I should've left her alone. Her parents haven't allowed me to contact her. But I couldn't *not* talk to her. See for myself that she was okay. *Just see her*. She's so beautiful, Axel."

She breaks off, her teeth sinking into her bottom lip. Before today, I wouldn't have touched that soft flesh, but here, now, in this room, I grant myself permission. Pressing my thumb against the tender curve, I gently pull it away and smooth my pad across the lightly dented, damp skin. My dick throbs, and I'd be the worst liar if I claimed I wasn't imagining how good it would feel to tap my swollen cockhead against this lush mouth before slowly, so fucking slowly, plunging into it. But I have a tighter rein on the beast, and picturing that is as far as I will allow myself.

Zenobia Hester isn't for me.

I'll have to settle for the gift of this small touch.

"Yeah, she is. She looks like you," I mutter.

Joy brightens her eyes, the gold glistening like freshly minted coins. "Thank you," she murmurs. "Thank you for coming today. And I'm sorry for lying to you about her identity. But thank you for not holding it against me."

"You're welcome."

Her hands slide up my back, and in the next moment, her arms are wrapped around me in a tight embrace that I should resist. If I had any integrity, I would pat her on the shoulder and then extricate myself. But I've crossed that boundary long ago. Fuck crossed it. I've torched it, then blew it up for good measure. So, the only thing left to do is fold myself around her and bend my head over hers, burying my face in her hair. Inhaling that cider and dew scent so deep in my lungs, it'll take a surgical procedure to remove it.

I'll allow this.

This is it, though.

But even as I think it, I don't believe it.

CHAPTER 10

watch the elevator doors close behind Axel, and even after he disappears from sight, I still stand there in the middle of the pediatric floor, stunned by the events that just happened in the on-call room.

I just confessed my deepest secret to someone I've known for days. *Days.* I was with James for *years*, and he never earned that trust. Part of me is still reeling, because, again, *what the hell just happened?* I have the rest of my shift to get through, but I'm exhausted from the emotional purging. Yet, I'm also… exhilarated, like a weight has been hauled off my chest. There'd been no judgement in Axel's eyes. No condemnation. Not even shock. And the man who can do an impressive mime routine like nobody's business uttered the perfect words to take away my guilt. Not completely. That task truly belongs to only me. But his calm, gruff, and no bullshit manner helped. God, it helped.

He'd offered me comfort when anyone else could've handed me censure.

So, what kind of person did it make me that while he'd hugged me I'd just wanted to climb him like a jungle gym and grind against that hard, big dick I'd ogled last night until I came so hard, exploding stars would have nothing on me?

I sigh.

It makes me an ungrateful, horny hot mess, that's what.

I can't remember the last time I'd felt so cared for, so protected, so *safe*… and so fucking turned on at the same time. Like, the whole hospital could be crumbling down around us and he would protect me with those wide shoulders and broad back, even while he fucked me into blessed oblivion.

Somehow, Axel Wright has transformed from the growly ogre under the bridge to the off-limits friend I'd love to fuck. Because there is no mistaking this—he is a friend. And I do want to fuck him.

But I can't.

Not only is he leaving the damn *country* in months, but I'm not even emotionally close to being involved with a man. James did one helluva job on my ability to trust, and if I'm brutally honest, my self-esteem. If I allowed it, Axel would just complete the wrecking that James started.

And I'm so fucking tired of being broken.

Of allowing myself to be a man's rest stop before he moves on to his final destination.

"Excuse me. Can I speak with you for a moment?"

I turn around, a smile automatically curving my lips, but it freezes as I meet the furious gaze of Danielle Mavis.

It's been over twelve years since I last saw her, but I immediately recognize her. How could I forget the face of the woman who I gave to raise my daughter as her own?

"Hello, Mrs. Mavis." I nod. "Of course."

Not wanting to have an audience of the whole floor for this conversation, I lead her toward the hall outside Bethany's room that's thankfully—miraculously—empty.

"You have some nerve," she hisses, her pretty face suffused with anger. "I told Sabrina Lorenzo that we weren't ready for Bethany to meet you yet. And then you pull this—" she waves a hand toward Bethany's hospital room door "—without our permission? I can have you fired, and I'm not completely certain I won't."

"You would be well within your right to do that," I say softly. "I'm sorry, Mrs. Mavis. I don't have any excuse, and all I can say is I'm sorry. I didn't think. I know it's doesn't excuse my actions, but I didn't tell Bethany who I am. She just thinks I'm her nurse."

"Oh, I know," Danielle sneers, crossing her arms over her chest. "That's the *only* reason I'm not in your supervisor's office right now. She didn't recognize your name, but I did. Bethany just thinks you're the nice nurse who brought her favorite artist by. Again, without her *parents'* permission. Who do you think you are?" she demands.

It's not just the fury that has me flinching; it's the hurt that thrums beneath it. And I understand. I violated boundaries. Yes, I birthed Bethany, but Danielle is her mother.

"I'm sorry," I whisper. "I'm so sorry." It's so inadequate, but it's all I have to offer her.

"It's not enough," she snaps. "Stay away from my daughter. I'm calling Sabrina and telling her the same thing.

And if you don't respect that, you'll not only be without a job but slapped with a restraining order. Leave her and us alone."

Danielle whips away, pushing open Bethany's door and disappearing inside the room. Leaving me shaking on the other side.

I fucked up.

And now I lost my only chance to be in my daughter's life.

Lost her before I truly even had her.

———

Hours later, Danielle Mavis's enraged words no longer ring in my head. That's mainly due to the bottle of Moscato I emptied by myself. Pleasantly buzzed, I lie back against the pillows in Gabrielle and Julian's guest room. Not my room. Not my home. My head rolls as I survey the pretty room, scrutinizing the elegant dresser and vanity, the gleaming hardwood floors, dark green area rug, small but lovely desk, and antique chair through bleary eyes. Nothing in here belongs to me except for the suitcases in the closet. I didn't even bother placing any of my things in the dresser drawers, not wanting to get too comfortable.

A Bachelor of Science in nursing, passing the licensed exam and thousands of hours in the emergency room in a challenging career I love, and what do I have to show for it?

I'm temporarily homeless.

I'm fiancé-less.

Any chance of connecting with my biological daughter is gone.

I'm alone. So fucking alone.

From the time I was sixteen, I've sacrificed for others. For my mother and grandparents. For my child. For James. Seldom have I been selfish. Never taking for myself. I've given my baby, my heart, even my independence for people I love, and have never asked for anything in return. And that's my fault. My problem.

Maybe I need to do the asking.

Maybe it's time I need to do the taking.

Just one thing for myself. I deserve it, dammit.

As soon as the thought stumbles through my mind, Axel flickers then solidifies in my head like an HD movie screen. Just earlier today I told myself he was off-limits, and I couldn't have him. But why not? It's not like I want to propose to him or even ask him to go steady. I just want to fuck. To scratch this relentless itch that he stirred when he showed up shirtless, tatted, golden, and gorgeous in Gabrielle's kitchen. Really, that makes it his responsibility to satisfy it.

If I go into this recognizing it for what it is—a no-strings-attached, dirty one-night stand—then what's the harm? We both get off, and I stop thinking. I stop feeling. I stop being anything but mindless with the pleasure my body has instinctively known his is capable of giving me from the moment I whipped around with a pot of grits in my hand.

That's it.

Carefully balancing my half-filled glass of wine in one hand, I scoot on my ass across the bed and shuffle across the room to the dresser where I dropped my phone before getting down to the serious business of getting wasted. I pick up the cell and glance behind me. Suddenly, the bed looms a little too far to travel, so holding my glass like the precious jewel it is, I sink to the floor, crossing my legs. A small, waaay-too-sober voice mutters that drunk texting is a really bad idea. But I shut that bitch up with a long, deep gulp of Moscato.

Pulling up my message app, I scroll to the last text I sent Axel when he messaged me this morning to let me know he'd arrived at the hospital. God, how was that just this today? So much had hap—*No! Nonono. We're not going there.* Just to make sure, here's more wine. I give the maudlin side of me another sip.

"There we go," I mutter, tapping on his name.

Our stream is very short. Just him informing me he's there and me saying okay. I stare at the new message bar.

Well, shit.

What should I say? Something like, *You down to fuck? Check yes, no, or maybe?* seems kinda, I don't know, sophomoric.

"Fuck it," I grumble. Minutes later, I stare down at what I've written, feeling my mouth pull into a stupid grin.

> Dear Axel,
>
> It is incredibly stupid to write this text while I'm drunk. But what's the saying? No gain, no pain. Or, no pain, no shame... Whatever. You know what I mean. And let's face it. There's no way I would be doing this if I was stone-cold sober. But since I'm plastered? To hell with it.
>
> I want you.
>
> I know. Crazy, right? Not only am I your temporary

roommate, but I'm a chatty nurse from Providence and you're a broody, commitment-phobe sculptor who communicates in grunts and single syllables. Not to mention, you're returning home to England in several weeks. And yet, from the moment you dragged me for being a Swiftie, I've wanted to climb you like my personal jungle gym.

There's no future for us. I'm not even sure I like you half the time. But that doesn't stop me from hungering for those same hands that bend and shape metal to bend and shape me. So, in all my drunken glory, I guess what I'm trying to say is if you want me, I'm yours. For the next few weeks until you return home and we resume our lives as before. No strings. No demands. No regrets.

So meet me in the kitchen where all this started.

Or don't.

It's your decision.

Not that it matters. It's not like I'm going to do something monumentally dumb and hit send on this text.

—Zenobia

I pick up my wine glass and toast myself. That's a bomb ass letter, if I must say so myself. Shaking my head, I tap the screen, shutting the phone off. Yeah, I'm shit-faced, but I'm not stupid or far gone enough to actually send that text. Damn sure felt good writing it, though.

Sighing, I tip the glass up and finish off the wine, part of me wishing I really had the lady balls to send it. To proposition Axel. Cackling to myself, I crawl over to the bed and pull myself up onto the mattress. Thank Christ I'm off tomorrow because I'm going to regret this in the morning.

Whether I mean the drinking or not going after what I want, I don't know.

I pass out before I can answer that question.

CHAPTER 11

ZENOBIA

God, I'm Your child. Why are you trying to take me out?

If God hears my prayer, He's not in the mood to answer. Which is a bit unreasonable. I mean, granted, it's been a minute since I've been in Bible study or a Sunday service, but I don't remember overindulging being among the Ten Commandments.

"Dammit!" Pain shoots from my stubbed toe, up my leg and straight to my heart. Bracing a hand against the bathroom doorjamb, I grasp the knot of my towel between my breasts with the other and try not to pass out from the throbbing agony that only increases the pounding in my head. "Fine," I grit out. "I'm sorry for the disrespect, God. My bad."

Geez, He answered *that one* quick.

Attempting to breathe through the pain, I limp down the hall and into the guest room, gingerly closing the door behind me. The fact that I'm feeling better than I did when I first woke this morning is something of a minor miracle. Now I only feel like day-old roadkill instead of fossilized roadkill. The Aleve I popped is kicking in and "human" seems achievable.

Still cautiously moving, I pull loose pajama pants up my legs, tying them at my waist and pull a tank on. Since I didn't bother putting on my sleep cap last night before passing out, I do what I can. Which isn't a lot, considering each pull on my tender scalp has pissed off nerve endings calling me everything but a child of God, regardless of what I claimed on my way out the bathroom.

Coffee. This calls for coffee.

Moments later, I shuffle into the kitchen, all my focus on the Keurig as if it's the one ring to rule them all and I'm seconds away from hissing, "My precious." Oh yeah. It's that deep.

Just as I open the cabinet door and grab a cup, the door to the garage opens. I glance over my shoulder.

"Hey, Axel." I set the mug on the counter and turn around, rummaging for a smile. Since I had a hot date with a bottle of Moscato last night, the last time we saw each other was at the hospital, and I haven't had a chance to tell him about— "Whoa. What the fuck?"

Axel stalks forward, brows lowered in a forbidding V, blue eyes almost glowing with intensity. My mouth drops open—I hear the small pop my lips make as they part—as he crosses his arms over his chest, grips the bottom of his shirt and drags it up and over his head, dropping it behind him. Long, blond hair tumbles to his powerful, bare, inked shoulders, hiding the shaved sides of his head. Lust, searing hot and immediate, blasts through me like a furnace ratcheted to Burn This Motherfucker Down. He doesn't stop, just keeps coming for me. And that's what he's doing. Coming for me. Hunting me down.

And though I'm not afraid of him, I still back up the scant inches between me and the counter until my butt smacks the edge. My palms hike up, seemingly of their own volition, and they meet naked, tight flesh. I groan. He groans. I don't know. But the dark, needy sound rents the air seconds before his big, long fingers tunnel through my hair, jerking my head back. Pain nips at my scalp, and I whimper at the minute sting, but it's different from earlier. Maybe because it's Axel's hands on me. That has to be it. He's the secret ingredient that turns pain into a curious blending of acute pleasure.

He presses his forehead to mine. "Yeah," he growls.

I blink. Yeah? What does he— *Oh shit!* The answer barrels into me like a runaway car with faulty brakes. Fast. Catastrophic. That one word unlocks my fuzzy memory. Wine. The text.

Hitting fucking send.

I groan again, but this time it isn't one of hunger, but mortification. I can't believe I sent that damn text. I'm an idiot.

"Axel—"

His mouth crashes over mine, and every word, every thought disintegrates under the heat of his kiss. Kiss? Ha. What a misnomer for this clash of lips, tongue, teeth and wills. It's wet. Wild. Raw. And so goddamn messy and greedy there's nothing beautiful about it. It's primal. It's necessary.

Blunt fingertips press against my scalp, tilting my head where he wants me, and I go, following his lead, trusting him to take me where he'll give me only the utmost of pleasure. And he does. He dives deeper, stretching my lips wider for his possession, licking at the roof of my mouth, the side of my cheek, sucking on my tongue. Axel leaves no part of me undiscovered, like I'm his greatest expedition and afterward he plans on staking a flag, letting everyone know he's been here. Letting them know he's claimed me.

My hands climb the hot, firm wall of his chest to tangle in his thick, silken hair. To clench. Hang on. I'm shameless in how much I want—*everything*. His tongue plunging in my mouth. His teeth nipping my swollen lips. His hands dominating me.

His cock branding my belly.

And still it's not nearly enough.

Hooking a leg around his muscular calf, I heave myself higher up his body, so his dick is notched closer to where I need it. Closer, but not there. Not riding my clit, spreading my folds. But just shortening the distance sends pleasure spiraling through me, ripping a moan from me. Has my sex clenching. As if it senses what it needs is just within its reach.

A large palm cups my ass, hauls me up, and oh God. My eyes damn near travel to the back of my head as that thick, long, fucking huge cock rubs over my pussy. I couldn't hold in the sob that trips out of me if I tried. And I don't even try. As a matter of fact, I might have muttered a prayer of thanks to him for giving this to me.

"This what you need, pet?" he damn near purrs, treating me to another rough roll of his hips. And another. And another. His dick drags over me, that thick head nudging then sliding over my clit through his sweatpants and my pajamas. "This? And this?"

I shudder, almost tipping over the edge with the added stimulation of his voice and his nasty grind. My pussy is no doubt dripping, turning the cotton pants into a soaked mess, and all I can do is nod, sinking me teeth into my bottom lip. And like he did yesterday, he thumbs it loose, soothing the flesh with his tongue instead of his finger.

"What else you need from me?" he rumbles against my mouth. "I'll give it to you. Anything, pet. Ask it."

That should be a demand, but it's almost as if he's begging me to do this for him. To request this of him so he can offer it to him. And it's a plea I can't deny.

"Slide your fingers under the straps of my top," I whisper, my eyes meeting his without wavering. It takes courage to do both—to not avoid that cerulean, piercing stare and to demand what I want. The latter more than the former. I'm not used to taking for myself, to asking for my needs to be satisfied. But with Axel, I sense that he's the mythical unicorn—the man who receives pleasure in giving it.

Abandoning my hair, he slowly lowers his hands to my shoulders and slips his fingers under my tank top's straps.

"Push them down my arms."

He follows my directions, gliding them down, his calloused fingertips grazing my skin, causing nerve endings to stand at strict attention and salute. I lift my arms and as the top lowers, baring my breasts, his eyes don't leave mine, and an odd twinge pinches my chest. But I ignore it, choosing to focus on the cool air brushing my flesh, beading my nipples to just-shy-of-painful points.

"Look at me," I whisper, hating the catch in my voice. Hating more that constriction behind my sternum that has yet to go away.

But only then does he drop his gaze, and my breath stalls in my lungs at the hunger that tautens the skin over his slashing cheekbones, at the hiss of greed that escapes his swollen, carnal lips. He flicks a look up at me, and if he reminded me of a Viking before, then it's Odin standing before me now, with lightning bolts flashing in his eyes. And the mere mortal that I am, I'm shaking, ready to kneel before him in total surrender and supplication.

When his scrutiny returns to my breasts, I breathe, "Kiss me. Suck me." A whimper that comes from a sharp wrench in my belly. "And don't be gentle."

He takes me at my word. He's not gentle. He's voracious. His big palms cup me, lifting me to his mouth, pushing my breasts together so he doesn't have to choose. He latches on to both nipples, sucking so hard I feel the pull high and deep in my pussy. My cry rebounds off the kitchen walls, rebounding and encamping around us. His tongue works the tips, lashing, circling, stabbing, flicking... Oh fuck, I can't keep up. I'm writhing like a mindless thing against him, arching, attempting to get closer. My fingernails scrape over his scalp, and he grunts, shoving his hips harder between my legs. He doesn't just use his mouth and hands to pleasure me. His whole body is a tool, a conduit, an instrument devoted to me.

"Axel," I whine. Yes, honest-to-God whine, and I don't care. Because that's how far I've regressed. I'll beg, plead, freaking kill for what he's giving me. No one's ever touched me with so much *starvation* before. So much need.

So much reverence.

"What else?" he growls, delivering one last suckle to my nipples then lifts his head, his thumbs rubbing circles over the beaded, wet peaks. "Tell me."

"Let me down."

He backs up, easing me off the counter and to the floor. It hits me that I should possess even the barest shreds of modesty as I sink to my knees in front of him, half-naked, shirt bunched around my waist. But I would be lying. I only feel reckless. Free. And for the first time in longer than I can remember… myself.

"I want you," I murmur, hooking my fingers in the band of his sweatpants and tugging them down to the tops of his thighs.

His cock bobs free, slapping his ridged abdomen. Dark blue veins rope his thick, long length, and my tongue aches with the desire to trace those pathways. I shamelessly moan and fist the wide base.

"Fuck," he barks, his voice dark, low, dangerous. "Zenobia, you don't…"

"I want you," I repeat, pumping the wider, lower half of him, slowly, my fingertips barely touching. I don't want to hear his sweet considerations telling me I don't have to do this for him. I know that already. It's what I need to do. No. What I *hunger* to do. "In my mouth. Down my throat."

His face hardens, an almost cruel slant curling one corner of his mouth. "Okay, pet." He buries his fingers in my curls, tugging my head back. "Open."

Eagerly, I obey. Although I asked for this, it's my will,

my pleasure to acquiesce. To surrender. And he doesn't make me wait. Covering my hands with one of his, he arrows his dick toward my mouth and feeds me his length. I rest my hands on his rigid, straining thighs and let him take over.

Inch by inch, he slides into me, pausing, waiting to see if he's too much. I shut my eyes. Because I didn't want this… tenderness. But he's giving it to me anyway. And damn, it's what I need. He knows me, understands what I need even when I don't. If he's taking my mouth like this, how will he be with my pussy? The thought sends a pulse of pure fire between my thighs, and I squeeze my thighs. But that only worsens the ache, the pleasure that borders on sexual agony.

"Jesus Christ, I almost can't look at you," he mutters, and my lashes lift, my gazing flying up to him. His is trained on my mouth, leaving me to stare at the expression that veers close to pain twisting his face. As if feeling my scrutiny, his eyes flick to mine, and his mouth quirks in a humorless grimace. "Watching you take my cock like a good, greedy little girl is going to unman me, pet," he murmurs. His hips pulse, pushing more of himself inside me until the head nudges the entrance to my throat. Then another little thrust that breaches it. "*Fuck.*"

He withdraws, bending over me, crushing a hard kiss to my mouth. His hand wraps around the front of my throat, his thumb massaging it.

"Not enough," I gasp against his lips, unable to remain still. Not with unrelenting claws of desire digging into me, demanding more of him. "Use me."

Electric bolts of light flare in his eyes and he jackknifes

over me, clasping my head between his palms and without warning, thrusting between my lips, over and over. Using me. Taking me. Fucking me.

I grab onto his hips, holding on as I suck at him, lick and exalt in this fury that he's unleashed on me. If his control has snapped, then I've taken the reins of it. I'm master of his pleasure. I'm his keeper, even though I'm the one on my knees. And as he penetrates my throat, snarling with the possession, I capitulate but also hold the power. Breathing is a theory. Hanging on, a survival instinct.

Only when he stiffens, my name a roar that careens around the room, his seed filling my mouth, my throat, do we both surrender. That huge body wilts over me, cradling my shoulders, shaking, vulnerable. But just for a moment. In the very next, I'm off the floor, in his arms, and the kitchen is in my peripheral vision. The garage speeds past me, and suddenly I'm in his apartment, the door slamming behind us, my back meeting the mattress, his woodsy and sex scent filling my nostrils.

I don't have time to even inhale a breath or call his name before my pajama pants are dragged down my legs and he's between them, his head buried in my pussy.

"Oh fuck. Oh fuck." My hands fly to his hair, tangling, clutching.

He eats me like he kisses me. Undisciplined. Wild. Like a starving, desperate man. I can't... *Jesus*. My back arches under the electric pulses of pleasure that strike me over and over, so fast, so violently, that part of me fears snapping in two under the pressure.

His tongue laps at my clit, stroking and seducing it even as he tortures it. Tortures me. I want to cry uncle, but the bit of me that remains sane, threatens to slap the shit out of myself if I dare. Axel is… relentless. It's as if my pleasure is his one goal in life, his one purpose for existing, and he's pursuing it with a God-almighty fervor that's inspiring and a little frightening.

Unable to not watch, I stare down my torso and have a front seat to him trailing that beautiful mouth through my folds, licking at them, nipping at them. He gives every part of my pussy due attention, worshipping me. And in this moment, I feel like a deity. Powerful and vulnerable. Strong and delicate.

He does this to me. Only him.

Palming my thighs, he spreads me wide and dips he head lower, sliding his tongue into my entrance… into my pussy. My lashes flutter, unable to stay open as a wave of lust rolls over me. A whimper escapes my throat and I thrust my hips up, silently but loudly demanding that mouth and a deeper, harder caress. And because he's Axel, because he can read me better than myself, he shifts a hand between my legs and buries two fingers inside me.

"Oh God," I cry out, twisting, curling into that touch. "Please," I beg. "Please, Axel."

"Whatever you want, pet," he promises, and proceeds to finger fuck me until I'm babbling praises, demands and pleas.

At some point, he must add another finger, because I'm fuller, it's a tighter fit and there's a burning, a stretching. And I'm so close to an orgasm, I might go crazy. Not letting up, he continues to pound into me, and the wet clap of his fist meeting my pussy, the flat of his tongue over my clit and the curl of his fingertips on that mystical place high up inside me answers every one of my prayers.

I splinter.

My scream razes my throat, but I can't stop as I explode into pieces. Rasps fill my ears as I return to myself, and it's then I realize that they don't just belong to me, but to Axel, too. He lies over me, his body covering me. We're both shaking so hard the bed quivers beneath us.

"Inside me," I manage, though my voice is so hoarse, I barely recognize it. "I need you inside me."

God, I do. Even though I just had the orgasm to end all orgasms, I still feel empty inside. I've never had his cock in my pussy, but I instinctively know, only he can fill this hollow ache.

Axel pushes off me, stripping his sweatpants from his body as he crosses to the dresser. Tugging open the top drawer, he removes a condom and, in record time, sheathes himself. Without tearing my eyes from the magnificent sight of him, I roll my poor tank top down my hips and legs, toss it to the side, and spread my legs. Welcoming him back.

He accepts, crawling onto the bed, his hair falling in a tangled waterfall of gold over his shoulders and into his face. He's a warrior god, and I'm his goddess. In here, in his bed, he's never treated me differently. And even as he crouches over me, the ends of his hair tickling my face and mingling with my darker curls, I'm... cherished.

Stupid. So stupid to interject any softer feelings other than lust and need into this room, into this fuck between friends. We're scratching an itch, just like my text said. No strings, no complications. And when it's over, it's over. He goes his way back to England, and I go mine back to my apartment across town.

Expecting more—even thinking about more—is just inviting trouble and needless heartache.

"Take me in, then," he orders, his lips brushing mine, his crystal gaze on mine.

Snaking a hand between us, I don't break our visual connection as I circle the base of his cock and guide him to my entrance. With my other hand, I cup a muscular ass cheek and press, notching him just inside me. Then, raising both arms above my head, I flatten my palms against his headboard and buck my hips, taking more of him.

I hiss, my eyes closing. His fingers had stretched me, prepared me, but dammit, they weren't his dick. His lips caress my forehead, cheekbones, arch of my nose, lips, chin. All the while, his hips pulse, much like when he fucked my mouth, gradually claiming my pussy.

He pauses, granting me time to become accustomed to the possession. Then, he gently thrusts again, pushing more of his dick inside me, stretching me. Branding me.

How long he repeats this erotic dance, I have no idea. At some point, I curl my arms around his wide shoulders, holding on, letting him completely fill me. And when he's fully seated within me, both of our pants break on air.

Part of me is afraid to move. Unsure if I will shatter. Can I withstand this pressure? And the other part? That part just doesn't want this to end. I've never been so connected to another person. Is this how God meant sex to be? Where not only bodies are intertwined, but souls? His heart beats against my chest, and I swear, mine follows the same rhythm; my breath mimics his pattern. Tears sting my eyes, and I pray I'm strong enough not to allow them to fall.

He can't suspect that I already violated the terms of the arrangement I stated in the text. He can't know that this suddenly isn't just sex for me.

"Look at me," he demands, voice gravel and silk.

But this time I can't obey. I shake my head, before pressing my face to the crook between his throat and shoulder. Maybe he senses not to push me—again, he's Axel—because he cradles the back of my head, brushing a kiss over my hair. Holding me close, he moves. Withdrawing until I'm almost empty except for just the head of his cock is lodged inside of my entrance. Then, I'm full of him again, his length marking every part of me, my muscles quivering around him. With his weight on me, I can't rock my hips, can't meet his strokes. All I can do is receive.

And he gives. God, does he give.

He fucks me with his whole body. His fingers fist my hair and gently, but firmly, tug my head back and he takes my mouth. His chest rubs over my nipples, taunting them with caresses that tighten them into firm points. Strong, powerful thighs spread mine wide, and each thrust grinds the base of his cock against my clit even as his length prods that spot that no man has reached before. Only him. Only Axel.

Why do I fear that's going to become a mantra for me?

Grabbing my hands, he tangles our fingers together, pressing them to either side of my head.

"Look at me," he orders again.

And this time, this time, I do. And whatever he sees there triggers something in him. His head jerks back, almost as if he recoils from it. But then, his mouth firms, flattens and he lowers his face over mine. "Give it to me, Zenobia. And don't you fucking hold back."

He releases one of my hands, grips my thigh, and hikes it higher, powering into me—harder, faster, all the while his eyes on me. Searching out whatever he demanded from me.

"Axel," I breathe. Or I try to. Drawing breath into my lungs is an exercise, a wish.

"Give. It. To. Me," he orders again.

And this time, I obey. The orgasm rips through me like a backdraft of ecstasy, incinerating me. My lips part, but unlike the first release, no sound emerges. I'm past that. Past sound. Past sight. Past feeling anything, *being* anything but pure pleasure.

At some point, Axel broke me.

And remade me into someone who I don't even recognize.

And as he shudders above me, pouring into the condom, and growling his release into my ear, I have just enough awareness left to be terrified.

CHAPTER 12

AXEL

"If you'd have told me when I woke up this morning that I would be eating eggs, sausage, and toast hours later, I probably would've given you both fingers. No," Zenobia says, pinching one eye shut and holding up her fork, "I would've first christened the toilet and *then* given you the fingers."

I stare at her, sitting with her legs crossed in the middle of my bed in a nest of tangled sheets and blankets that still holds the scent of our sex. Plate balanced on her thighs, she scoops up more scrambled eggs that I cooked for her and slips them between her lips. It probably makes me a bit of a caveman that pride balloons in my chest as I watch her eat food that I cooked for her. Or that I'm more concerned with her hunger being satisfied than cleaning my plate. But I can't deny the truth. I want her full, content. Wanting for nothing.

"Here." I pick up her cup of coffee of the bedside table and pass it to her.

She sets down her fork and eagerly accepts it, humming. Her lashes lower as she sips, but they snap back open, surprise flaring in the golden-brown depths.

"Three creams and one sugar," she murmurs. "Just the way I take it. You paid attention."

I don't answer, but of course, I did. There isn't much about her that I haven't noticed. Like the small, faint, sickle-shaped scar that runs under her jaw. Or that when she's trying not to smile, her throat works likes she's physically swallowing laughter. Or when she finds something incredibly idiotic, she quietly mouths, *wow*.

And when she comes, her tight pussy clamps down on my dick like one of my table vises, and her eyes go from golden to the darkest amber.

She's fucking gorgeous.

And even more so, now that I know the greedy sounds she makes as she swallows my dick; the scent of her skin, damp from twisting under me; that stunning, thick body begging for more of me. Now that I know this hungry, relentless *craving* inside me isn't one-sided.

When I received that text from her last night, I'd thought she'd had me right up the garden path and had waited for a follow up message with the punch line. But no other text had arrived, and as I read it over—and over and over—again, lust crawled through me, gaining power, speed, and strength until I stalked to the kitchen, ready to take her up on her offer. Willing to enter into another doomed, tempo-rary whatever-the-fuck-it-is knowing she would walk away, and in some way, I would fail or disappoint her.

I always did.

All I had to do was glance behind me at the dry bones of my relationships littering my path to confirm that truth. My parents. Julian. Trish. My ex, who'd only been the latest in a short but doomed list of exes.

This thing had no good ending, and if I'd stopped thinking with my dick for half a second, I'd end it right now.

"Earth to Axel." She tips her head and studies me with the intensity of the hottest torch. "What're you thinking?"

"Why'd you send that text?" The question barrels out of me before I can corner it and wrestle the fucker back into whatever emo hole it skulked free of. But shit, it's out there now. And I want to know.

She sighs, shifting the nearly empty plate from her lap and handing both it and the mug toward me. I accept the dishes, not taking my gaze from her as I set them on the bedside table. Zenobia pulls her thighs to chest, tugging my T-shirt over her legs and crossing her arms over her knees.

"Honestly?" She scoffs, wrinkling her nose. "Don't you hate when people say that? No, lie to me."

She huffs out a laugh, rocking a little.

"I was drunk as hell."

My gut clenches, and ice slides through my veins. "You didn't mean any of that."

Her mouth twists into a smile that isn't quite a smile. "Oh, I meant it. Every word. Now did I mean to send it is a different question."

She thrusts a hand in her curls, closing her eyes, her lips soundlessly moving. "Alcohol gave me the courage to type out what I'd never have the lady balls to say to your face in real time. But it also had me hit send when I didn't intend on going that far. This"—she flicks a hand back and forth between us—"isn't the smartest of ideas, Axel."

Seconds ago, I'd said the same thing to myself. But now, I keep my mouth shut. Because the idea of uttering anything that would keep me from getting inside her again has every primal instinct in me roaring in outrage and horror.

"Why were you wankered?"

A faint smile flirts with her mouth. "Wankered? God, I love you British." All hints of amusement disappear from her lips and voice, and shadows enter her eyes, muting the gold.

I don't think. Don't question the wisdom of the gesture or the meaning she could assign to it. I just hold out my hand. "You need me?"

She stares at my palm, and just when I'm about to lower my arm back to my side, she lunges forward, grabbing ahold as if she's a shipwreck victim grasping for a lone piece of driftwood. In a matter of seconds, she's in my arms, her firm arse cradled against my thighs and cock, her head pressed to my chest. Those curls, which I'm beginning to suspect I have an unhealthy obsession with, graze my throat.

I don't pressure her. We sit there, my arms wrapped around her, lending her whatever she requires to get through these next few minutes.

"After you left," she finally begins, her words whispering over my skin, "Bethany's mother found me. She..." Her breath hitches, and I stroke a hand up her back, cupping the back of her neck. "She knew who I was and ordered me to stay away from Bethany. That if I tried to contact her again, she'd have me slapped with a restraining order and fired."

A tremble quakes through her body, and I absorb it, shelter her with my body, though I can't protect her from the hurt already inflicted on her. This is a decades-old wound, and there's nothing I can do to heal it.

Helplessness surges within me, anger quickly nipping at its heels. I want to fix this for her, and it's gutting me that I can't.

"Last week, I'd sent a request to the Mavises through my adoption counselor to meet Bethany. They'd turned me down. One of the terms of the semi-open adoption was that not only do I receive pictures and letters from them about Bethany, but that I would one day get to meet her at their discretion. Since she's about to be a teenager, I thought it might be a good time. They didn't. But now..." Her shoulders hunch, and she curls into me. "Now, they'll probably never agree to let me meet her before she's of age. I fucked that up and have nobody to blame but myself."

"Stop," I order in voice that's far harsher than I intended.

She jolts a little, but my arm around her tightens, cradling her closer and squeezing her nape in assurance. Dragging in a breath, I try to slow the sudden thudding of my heart, realizing she can probably hear it with her ear pressed to my chest.

"Axel."

I squeeze her again, gentler, but the message is clear. *Hold on. Give me a minute.*

After several moments, I try again, staring straight ahead at the wall. "We make do with what we have left."

She stirs, and her head tips back—or she tries to tip it back, but I don't allow her. I tuck it under my chin. I can't say this and stare into those honeyed eyes too.

"When my brother Blake died, my life changed forever. The happy, idyllic life I'd known had been obliterated, like a bomb had been dropped on it and we were left with the wreckage, the rubble. Then we were tasked with scraping it together to form this new… existence."

Her arms slide around me, hands hot on my back. Small, gentle kisses are brushed over my chest, directly over my still pounding heart.

"What I'm telling you is we make do with what we have left. I turned further into my art, took to metal." There's a magic, a sort of resurrecting power in taking the forgotten, the rubbish and, for all intents and purposes, the dead, and birthing new creations. "And you, having given up your child, maybe you poured that love to caring for others with your nursing. And when your child came into hospital, right or wrong, you made do with that moment of time you had with her. Let it go, pet. Not even God can change the past and let the future take care of itself. Especially since I've learned in the worse of ways that it's not promised to us."

This time, she doesn't let me stop her from leaning back. Doesn't prevent my arms from restricting her movement. Zenobia shifts on top of me, straddling my thighs, the heat from her sex pressing against my cock through my sweatpants. But I barely feel it as I grip her waist. Because she cups my face, tilting me head back, and stares into my eyes.

And only the intensity, the beauty of that golden gaze can compete and win over the power of her pussy.

"I'm sorry about your brother, Axel." She skims her fingertips over my eyebrows. The bridge of my nose. My cheekbones. My mouth. Then retraces those same paths with her lips. My work has been praised before, but I've never personally felt revered. I can no longer say that. "And I'm sorry that the only comfort you had was art and not family."

Shock ripples through me, and my instinctive reaction is push her away. To reject her and that statement—no matter how accurate it is. It's why I need away from her. Because the truth literally hurts.

"No," she whispers, locking her arms around my neck, squeezing her thighs to my hips. Yes, I could remove her, but it would require force, and that I can't do. And fuck. She knows it, takes advantage of it. Her lips graze the rim of my ear, her warm breath a sensual caress that, dammit, has a hard shudder passing over me. "I'm not going to let you push me away. Too many people have let you be alone in your head, in your art. I'm forcing my way in, Axel."

She raises up, lowers an arm and reaches between us. In seconds, she has my cock freed from my pants and is sinking, sinking... Jesus, she's taking me inside her liquid, tight heat and that shudder transforms into a quake. My grip on her hips must be bruising, but I can't ease up, can't let go.

"I'm so sorry you lost the brother you loved."

She lifts over me, dragging her grasping pussy up my dick, then in an excruciating slow glide, slides back down, claiming me, embracing me. A groan rips from my throat, and I squeeze my eyes shut against the exquisite and punishing pleasure. I'm bare—the knowledge slams into me like a sledgehammer. With a condom, the kiss of her sex had been pure heaven. Without that barrier, it's a blinding, brutal combination of beautiful heaven and fiery hell.

"And I'm sorry that you also lost the world you knew. You deserved more. This beautiful, gifted, broken heart deserved more."

She places a sweet kiss below my ear. In direct contrast to the filthy caress her pussy delivers to my cock as she rides me. Breath catching, she cups my shoulders, gently pushing me back against the mattress and falling over me. Her curls are an enticement I can't deny, and I bury my fingers in them, tangling, dragging her even closer to me. For moments, nothing but the sounds of our fractured moans, the slap of our damp skin and the wet suck of her pussy fill my room.

"I'm in, Axel," she breathes, her gorgeous face twisted in a grimace of pleasure that makes her even more beautiful. "I'm in, and you won't even be able to push me out."

I grind my teeth together, trapping anything that would make a prison break from me without my permission. Least of all, a demand of a promise. That she swears to this even though the very nature of this relationship we've entered is temporary.

But I don't say it. Still, her words snap the rapidly unraveling threads of my control. Wrapping one arm around her waist, I pump into her clenching sex and snake the other between us, easily finding her clit. I pinch the engorged flesh, rubbing it once, twice, and that's all it takes to have that sweet, tight core clamp down on me, milking my cock, coaxing me to follow her over the edge.

And I give in.

Electric pulses race up and down my body, seizing the base of my spine, sizzling in the soles of my feet. But before I totally surrender to the siren's call of oblivion, I wrench her off me, fist my dick, and stroke, cum spurting out of me. My back arches with the hot pour of it, and fuck, for a moment, I don't think it's going to stop. I don't want it to stop. And as she collapses against me, I don't want this to stop either.

Which is foolish wishful thinking, even for me.

Because as I told Zenobia, nothing is promised.

Everything has to come to an end.

CHAPTER 13

ZENOBIA

"No." I groan, slapping at Axel's bedside table to shut off the alarm. "More sleep."

The heavy, muscular arm around my waist tightens. Axel shifts behind me, but then stills again. Something I've learned about him over the past four days since we've started this little arrangement: once asleep, it takes a train roaring through the room to wake him up.

Another thing I've discovered?

He doesn't have an alarm clock.

Confusion trickles through me, and one of my eyes peels open as the sound that penetrated my subconscious reaches me again. Is that…? No, couldn't be…

Holy shit! It is.

"Dammit!" I jackknife up and scramble from under his weight and the blankets. "Axel," I hiss while searching the floor of his apartment for my discarded shorts and shirt. "Axel!" I dare to whisper-shout as loud as I can. Tugging my clothes up my legs, I lean over the bed, cup his shoulder and shake his big frame. "Wake up."

He blinks, his fuzzy blue eyes meeting mine.

"Julian and Gabrielle are home."

Seconds after I drop that bomb on him, the sleep clears from his gaze, and he frowns, sitting up. "What?"

"Julian. Gabrielle. The people who are letting us stay under their roof?" I pull my shirt over my head. "They're here. Back from vacation four days earlier than scheduled. *Shit*."

I'm a fucking toddler trying to find the right holes in this thing. Heart pounding in my chest, I inhale a deep breath and waste precious seconds untangling the top and poking my arms through the correct sleeves.

"They can't find me here."

Here being in his apartment with him.

"Fuck." He scrubs a hand over his face, the abrasion of skin skating over his beard echoing in the room.

"Exactly."

I hurry across the floor and grasp the doorknob. Disappointment and a sudden ache blooms behind my sternum. Both drive me back to the bed. Diving on it, I crush my mouth to his for a quick, hard kiss. Fuck morning breath. We're losing the idyllic haven from the world we created between us, for us. And I'm mourning it. Because with Julian, Gabrielle, and their family's return, that's coming to an end.

Pushing myself off the bed again, I retrace my steps and pull the door open before I can crawl back among those covers and submit to the urge to hide under them. "I'll try to head them off in the kitchen. Give me a minute before you come out."

Without waiting for his response, I slip out, closing the door behind me, not allowing myself one last glance. I'm too weak for that. Silently, I pad across the garage and pause in front of the kitchen entrance, hand on the doorknob. When I don't hear voices on the other side, I gingerly twist the knob and push. Exhaling, I step in, quietly closing the door behind me and scurrying to the coffee maker as if I'd been there along about to mainline the first hit of caffeine. My pulse is racing like I already indulged in something stronger.

I grab a mug and K-cup, pop the pod in, and just as I hit the button to start the coffee brewing, Gabrielle appears in the kitchen.

"Z!" My friend rushes across the room and envelopes me in a hug. The weight in my chest hasn't eased, but delight still fills me at seeing my girl. I've missed her something fierce at work. Off work, too. "I've missed you."

She leans back, brown eyes sparkling, her dark brown locs swinging. At thirty-eight, she's a decade older than me, but I swear, she looks younger. That's what being happy and confident in yourself, being in complete love and the mother of the best kids ever will do for a person.

"I've missed you, too." I grin, pulling her in for another hug. "You scared the shit out of me, though. What're you guys doing home so early? Was the happiest place on earth not quite as happy?"

I twist and grab my coffee, glancing at her over my shoulder with an arched eyebrow.

She snorts. "Shut up and fix me one of those, please."

Chuckling, I pass her mine and retrieve another mug and K-cup.

"We found out that Xavier has a science project coming up that he can't miss, even though it wasn't included on the list of assignments given to him before we left. It's worth 50 percent of his grade, so we packed up and here we are." She sighs, and leaning forward whispers, "Can I be a bad mother and admit that I want to send his science teacher a big ass fruit basket? I was so ready to come home. If I had to go down Space Mountain one more time, Donald or Mickey was going to get junk punched."

I laugh just as Julian strides into the kitchen. "I heard that, luv, and you should be ashamed. I don't even know how I can stand to look at you right now," he chides in his crisp accent, but the adoration that shines from his hazel eyes as he gazes at his wife makes a lie of that statement. Even after six years together, five and a half years of marriage, and twins, these two still appear seconds away from jumping each other.

I eye the kitchen table with suspicion. Yeah, I'd rather not know what secrets it has. I ate off of it, after all.

"Zenobia, my darling, have you missed me?" He spreads his arms wide, and yes, he's my best friend's husband, but still, I get why all the nurses call him Dr. Sexy Pants.

Tall, beautiful, bald and bearded with piercing hazel eyes, gorgeous ebony skin, chiseled jaw, and a body that doesn't quit, he's movie star handsome. Yet, he does nothing for me. I mean, I've always looked at Julian as a friend. It has nothing to do with a recently discovered fascination for men who resemble Viking warriors with voices made of grit and whiskey.

"I sure did." I go into his arms, hugging him tight. "But I have to admit without you around, the nurses have been more productive. No Dr. Sexy Pants to drool over."

"God, I hate that name," he grumbles as Gabrielle and I snicker.

"Pop, Cecee, and Bree won't let me help them unpack. They said only you can do it." Xavier, Gabrielle's thirteen-year-old son from her first marriage, walks in, Julian and Gabrielle's four-year-old twins Celia and Breanna trailing behind him. His world-weary tone belongs to someone who has suffered all the indignities of life and is seriously put out by them. "Hey, Z!"

I adore this kid, and though he's approached that age where he's too cool to hug, I don't let that stop me from grabbing him close and smacking a kiss on top of his head. "Hey, Xavier! You enjoy your trip?"

"It was cool."

Oh yeah. *Such* a thirteen-year-old boy.

"I mean, it was al— *Whoa! Thor!*" he shouts, his teenage cool suddenly abandoning him.

I don't need to glance toward the garage entrance to guess Axel had entered the room. His presence crackles and leaps over my skin like my body has been plugged into a wall socket.

Jesus Christ. Don't scare the kids, I silently scold my nipples which threatened to bead under my shirt.

"Sorry to disappoint, but not Thor, son." Julian coughs, covering a laugh. He affectionately tousles Xavier's hair, who still stands, mouth hanging open, gaping at Axel. "Axel. Good to see you, mate."

Julian strides over and grabs him up in a hug. For a moment, Axel doesn't return the embrace—his huge, muscled arms remaining down at his sides—but then, almost awkwardly, he lifts them and pats Julian on the back. If Julian notices Axel's discomfort, he doesn't reveal it or comment. Instead, he shifts away, his hand remaining on one of Axel's shoulders.

"Come on. I'd like you to meet my family. This starstruck guy over here is my son Xavier. These two little angels are my girls Celia and Breanna. And the tall angel is my wife Gabrielle. Everyone, this is my friend, Axel Wright."

"Cheers," Axel says, jerking his chin up.

Cecee and Bree stare up at him, eyes round, and poor Xavier. I'm stuck between wanting to pat him on the head and running for my phone and snapping his picture so I can torment him with a picture of his Cool Point Epic Fail for life.

"It's nice to finally meet you, Axel," Gabrielle greets, trying and not succeeding in hiding a smile at her kids' reactions to him.

But who can blame them? He's… God. Him. I've just left his bed, and I'm nearly struck dumb by the sight of him with his golden hair slapped up in a messy bun and clothed in a wrinkled T-shirt that hugs his muscular torso. Faded jeans drape off his hips and cling to thick, powerful thighs. I've seen the man naked, so in clothes, his magnetism should at least be a wee bit muted. But no such luck.

God, I wish there was a dial at his back where he could

just switch that hotness from nuclear to regular ol'
phenomenal.

At least then it would be easier to not pant after him in
front of witnesses.

One peek at him, though, reveals he's not experiencing
that issue. He stares at me, and that quick I'm caught in that
electric blue trap. *There are kids in the room*, my brain
screams in warning. *Abort! Abort!* But apparently, my
vagina has shanghaied this ship, because my body is in full
rebellion, and I can't look away. Images of what he did to
me just hours ago download to my brain, and my lungs
seize, my stomach clenches and my sex quivers.

I'm in trouble.

The peal of a familiar ringtone saves me from complete
humiliation. Jerking my gaze from him, I glance toward
Xavier, who is holding my phone toward me.

"I forgot to tell you, Z. Your phone was ringing on my
way down here. Twice. Whoever's calling must really want
to contact you."

"Thanks."

I meet him halfway, keeping my attention focused on
him, but not before skimming over his father. More specifically, the narrowed, speculative gaze of his father. Well, shit.
Something tells me Julian didn't miss that little byplay
between Axel and me. I smother a sigh. Not that I have to
explain myself to him or seek his permission seeing as I'm a
fully-grown woman, but he and Gabrielle *did* offer me their
home. Yeah, I can't touch that decision until after coffee.

Accepting the phone, I hit the accept button on the
screen. "Hello."

"Morning. Is this Zenobia Hester?"

"Yes, this is her."

"Great. This is Greg, the super at your apartment building."

Surprise flares inside me, followed by a heavy coil of foreboding. Good God, what now? "Hey, Greg. Is something wrong with the repairs?"

"On the contrary," he assures me. "I'm calling to let you know we finished with everything ahead of schedule. If you'd like to move back in tomorrow, you can."

"Wow, that's… great." Isn't it? It is. Then why aren't I happy? My gaze flicks to Axel, who's sitting at the breakfast bar, his back stiff. "Thanks for letting me know."

"No problem. Have a great rest of your day."

I end the call and stare at the cell. Julian and Gabrielle returning home early. My apartment ready ahead of time. It's like the universe is telling me this no-strings affair has reached its expiration date. I mean, I *knew* that it had to. Just not so soon. Not before I had my fill of him.

As if that could ever happen. Wasn't it you telling him you're behind those walls of his and he won't ever be able to push you out?

Oh, shut up. I can't be held responsible for what I say during sex.

Jesus. I pinch the bridge of my nose. I'm officially losing it.

"Z? Everything okay?" Gabrielle asks, settling a hand on my shoulder.

"Great." I force a smile, that from her arched brow, I don't think is fooling her. "That was my building super. My apartment is ready, and I can get out of your hair sooner than I thought."

"Oh, that's awesome. Not that we want to get rid of you." She smiles. "But I know how you've hated being displaced. This will be getting some normalcy back."

"True."

Axel's stare is like a brand on my skin, but I don't look in his direction. Instead, I return to the coffee machine and busy my hands with making a cup. Maybe by the time it's brewing, I'll have convinced myself this jagged-edged disappointment in my chest is due to not having a whole house at my disposal and not because my no-feelings-no-strings affair with Axel ended before it really even had a chance to begin.

Yes. That's why.

God, I'm such a shitty liar.

CHAPTER 14

"Zenobia." Brenda Shannon approaches the nurses' station where I'm charting, her usually stern face softened by the concern swimming in her brown eyes. "You have a visitor. You have a break coming up in twenty minutes. Why don't you go ahead and take it now?"

"O-okay," I stutter, frowning. But then she steps to the side, and my gaze lands on the person standing behind her. Thank God I'm sitting. Shock blindsides me and would've knocked me on my ass.

As it is, I grip the desk, steadying myself, and blink. Because I can't believe my daughter is here.

"Bethany?" I whisper. "What are you doing here?"

"I came to see you." Bethany glances at Brenda, then back at me. "I know who you are."

The announcement plows whatever breath I managed to maintain out of my lungs. "I-I—"

I can't speak. Can barely think.

"You two should probably take this to the cafeteria," Brenda suggests. She circles the desk and cups my elbow in a firm grasp, helping me to my feet. Even offering me support as I take a few precious moments to ensure I don't fall on my face. "I'm going to put you down for PTO."

I can only nod and somehow manage to stumble around the desk and meet Bethany on the other side. She tilts her head back to meet my gaze. *I know who you are.* Her words rebound inside my head on an endless loop as we stare at each other, seemingly for the first time. And in a way it is. It's the first time we're meeting one another in honesty—as biological mother and daughter.

"Do you want to go to the cafeteria so we can talk?" I ask.

She nods and ten minutes later, we're seated at a table in a corner of the large atrium, her with a hot chocolate and me with a large coffee, because it's so needed. Neither of us sip, though. We're too busy studying each other—again.

"I don't have your eyes." She scrunches her nose. *That,* she totally gets from me.

"No, your biological father had hazel eyes."

"Does he know about me?"

I hesitate, unsure how much of this conversation we should be having without her parents here. I've violated enough of their trust. And I can't help but notice that she's dressed in a uniform with a book bag slung over the back of her chair.

Stiffening, I cock my head, narrowing my eyes. "Bethany, do your parents know you're here?"

Now she hesitates, but after a moment, she grudgingly admits, "No. I skipped school and took the bus here."

Oh shit. "Bethany—"

"I don't care if I get in trouble." Her mouth sets in a mutinous straight line and anger flashes in her green-brown eyes. "If I asked them if they would bring me to see you, they would've said no. And don't bother telling me I don't know that. I overheard you and Mom arguing outside of my hospital room. She told you to stay away from me. It's not fair." She shakes her head, her hands fisting beside her cup. "She should've asked me if I wanted to meet you. Because I do—I have for a while. I want to get to know you. And I knew the only way that was going to happen was if I came to see you myself."

My heart expands it's about to burst from my chest. But a second later, caution whispers through my head. Damn, this is bad. I can't go behind the Mavises' back again—I just can't. But the thought of rejecting her... My stomach roils and bile races for the back of my throat. No, that I can't do either.

"Okay, I understand the why, but skipping school to do it? And going behind your parents' backs? Can't sign off on it." I hold up a finger when she parts her lips to object. "But I get it. And not only would I be a bald-faced liar but a bad one if I said I'm upset you're here."

Her mouth pops closed at my admission.

"Still," I continue, "you need to call your parents. Now. Let them know where you are and to meet us here in the cafeteria. Bethany, your mom had every right to tell me to stay away from you. I shouldn't have approached you without her and your father's permission first. I'm your biological mother, but they're your parents, and I didn't respect that. I won't make that mistake again. So, give them a call, and let's see if, maybe, there's a way to work this all out."

She chews on her bottom lip for a moment, staring down at the table. Then, huffing out a drawn-out sigh, she twists around and removes her phone from her backpack.

"Okay, fine." She taps the screen, then holds the cell to her ear. Eyes meeting mine, she says, "Hey, Mom. I have something to tell you."

I inhale.

And it seems like forever before I let it go.

AXEL

Pride is an insidious emotion. It can fill a person with confidence but in the next instant trip that same person up and send him tumbling arse over head into failure. Yet, switching off the welding torch and removing my protective gear, studying the work I just finished, I can't deny it's pride that swells inside my chest.

Lady Amalthea.

Her ethereal figure is captured by metal honed so delicately, it appears as if one touch could snap it in half. The flowing dress. The long, gossamer strands of hair. The elfin-shaped face. The star on her forehead. She stands, hands clasped to her breasts, head tipped back, as if gazing up at the sky, searching for answers about this strange, new world she's been thrust into.

Objectively, it's one of the best pieces I've done.

Subjectively, it's fucking brilliant.

I drag in a breath, then cough, wincing at the wheeze and rattle in my chest. Dammit. My asthma has been fucking with me the last couple of days, and I've been sucking on my inhaler more than usual. Like now. Digging into my pocket, I retrieve my inhaler and take two puffs. My chest loosens, and I inhale again. Thank Christ this one is deeper and doesn't have as much of a wheeze. Out of curiosity, I glance at the back to see how many puffs I have left. Six. Well, shit. I didn't even realize it'd gotten that low. I need to call in a refill tomorrow or see if Julian can get a new one for me. The way I've been sucking on this thing, I can't afford to be without a prescription on hand. I damn sure can't afford to be down with an attack. I have too much work ahead of me. Right now, I'm good for the number of pieces planned, but any hiccup could set me back.

I hate hiccups.

Threading my fingers through my beard, I head across the warehouse toward the room that was probably some manager's office once upon a time. Now it's my employee breakroom for one where I stowed a mini-refrigerator, small table, and chair. Moments later, I reenter the workshop with an ice-cold bottle of water, and a knock on the rear door echoes through the room. Frowning, I don't move to answer it.

Who the fuck could that be? And at seven o'clock at night? Not Nate, because I told him I'd find my own way home. With Zenobia moving back to her apartment, there's no point in me heading back to Julian's house anytime soon. For what? To be reminded she's not there? To lie down in sheets that carry her scent? To eat in a kitchen that holds memories that I need to start forgetting?

I'd rather work myself until I'm too tired to do anything but shower and get knocked the fuck out.

Another knock reverberates through the workshop.

Shit. Whoever it is isn't going away. At least not until I tell them to.

Fingers tightening around the water bottle until it gives an ominous crack, I stalk across the workshop. When I reach the door, I shove it open. "What?"

"Uh, hi to you, too?" Zenobia smiles up at me. "Can I come in, or are you just going to stand there and growl at me all night?"

I shift backward, allowing her space to move past me. Her apple and earth scent teases me, and yeah, there's a possibility she could glance back and catch me closing my eyes and savoring it like some pervert or stalker, but I chance it. Closing my eyes, I breathe her in, thankful I just took my inhaler so I can capture a lungful of that spicy, earthy fragrance.

Christ, I've missed her.

It's only been over twelve hours since I've seen her—over twelve hours since I've been buried inside her—and I hurt for her.

But what we agreed to is over. As soon as Julian returned home with his family, it signed the death warrant on that bargain. Which is fine. It wasn't meant to be long-term anyway. No emotions. Just scratching a desperate itch. Satisfying an animal jerk.

Nothing more.

Doesn't explain why I'm over here fucking mainlining her scent.

"I stopped by Julian and Gabrielle's to pack up my stuff and saw you weren't there, so figured you must still be here working." She stops by my welding table, staring down at the piece I just finished. "Oh shit," she breathes, reaching out a hand, but then snatches it back. "This is gorgeous. I'm sorry, Axel. It's rude to look at your work without asking, isn't it? Hell, it's probably rude just to drop by unannounced. I wasn't thinking."

"What's wrong?" Because she's nervous again. And I thought we were past that. I've had my face in her pussy. How can she possibly still be nervous around me?

"Nothing." I frown, and she holds a hand up, palm out and chuckles softly. The sound skims over my skin like a sensual caress, and I shift, restless. "Seriously, there is nothing wrong. Everything is absolutely... right. I have the best news, and you were the first person I wanted to share it with. But when you weren't at the house, I impulsively decided to come and find you. Sorry if I intruded on your work."

"You don't have to apologize to me, Zenobia." Not when she's given me a gift. Seeking me out, wanting me to be the person she shares with? That might not seem like much to her. But to me? It's as fragile, as priceless as the most coveted artwork.

"Right." She turns back to the sculpture and studies it for another long moment. "There's such beauty inside you, you know that? It just amazes me."

I stare at her, shock paralyzing my vocal cords. Where the hell did that come from? Before I can ever try to form a reply—but fuck, what the hell do I say to that?—she smiles at me.

"Bethany came to the hospital looking for me today. Apparently, she overheard the conversation between her mother and me last week. She was curious about me and wanted to meet me as her birth mother instead of her nurse."

"Wasn't expecting that," I say, scanning her face. But unlike that day in my bed, there isn't any pain. Just a quiet joy and… peace. "I'm guessing everything went okay?"

She laughs again, and it has a bit of a hard edge. "Not at first. She'd played hooky to see me. I made her call her parents, and they were not happy, as you can well imagine. When they arrived at the hospital, initially they wanted no part of a conversation with me. They wanted to pick her up, take her home, and have no further contact with me. But Bethany was adamant. She's an amazing kid."

"She's her mother's daughter." To me, it was pretty damn obvious.

She smiles. "Thank you for saying that. But I credit all that to the Mavises. Sure, she has my DNA, my features, and some of my mannerisms, but that confidence, strength and yes, knowledge of being loved and accepted? That's all due to the wonderful parents they are. Now, I believe I can take credit for *that* since I chose them for her."

Her smile momentarily flashes wider into a grin, but then it dims, softens into something more thoughtful, wistful.

"Like I said, Bethany was insistent, and we all ended up sitting down and talking. And they *listened* to her when she said how she just wanted to get to know me. And not as a mother, because she has one of those. But as a friend. She's curious about her history, where she comes from. And I respect that. And so did her parents. They finally agreed to allow her to meet up with me—with them present—and gradually introduce me into her life."

"Then why're you nervous?"

"And here I thought I was hiding it so well." She snorts, dipping her head. When she lifts it, the shadows in those golden-brown eyes gut me. "I'm scared," she rasps. "What if I mess this up like I did the first time? Or what if she does get to know me and is disappointed? I'm not who she thought I was? Or I don't hold up to the image in her head? Or what if she's mad at me for giving her up in the first place? I don't want to fuck this up. It's too important."

I open my arms.

And she flies into them.

For long moments, we stand there, wrapped in each other. Her heart thuds, vibrating through my body, and I tighten my embrace, wishing like hell I could absorb each and every shiver that ripples through her. Several more minutes pass while I gather my thoughts, parse through them, discard them as too trite, too pat. Truth. All I have for her is truth. Even if it's too discombobulated, too raw. Too passionate.

Too revealing.

"When I first saw you," I murmur into her curls, "I hurt with the need to sculpt you. It roared at me so loud that I almost couldn't think, couldn't hear. Even when you hit me with that slop you call food."

She huffs out a laugh, but it's muted, because she's gone

still. As if she's clinging to every word that's coming out of my mouth.

"I needed to capture all that beauty and militance in metal so years from that moment, people would lay their eyes on you and be fucking *awed*. Like I was."

Her sharp, indrawn breath echoes in the room, and her nails dig into my back past my overalls and T-shirt.

"An Amazon. That's how I would sculpt you. That's how I would immortalize her. With a helmet on top of these thick curls, armor on this petite but powerful body, and a sword in your delicate but strong hand. Because that's how I saw you, and it's how I still see you. Fearless. Fierce. Indomitable. I'm not saying all those things you fear won't happen. But I am saying if they do, I have no doubts you'll conquer them, because that's what you do, Zenobia. You're a warrior."

"Fuck."

I snap my head back, because—yeah. I'm not a man who's comfortable with words, but were they *that* bad?

"I'm also an ugly crier," she whispers, then sniffs.

Amusement bubbles up in my chest, and I lean back, shifting my hands to cup her face but she dips her head, dodging me. But I don't allow her to. I palm her cheeks, tilt her head back and stare down into the face that I suspect will haunt me even after I return home months from now.

Tears glisten in her eyes and track down her face.

"No one has ever said anything so lovely to me before." She turns into my hand and kisses my palm. "No one has ever seen me like you do."

"Fuck them," I mutter, kissing those tears, tasting them, claiming them.

She laughs, grasping my wrists and leaning her head back farther. When my lips brush the corner of hers, she presses her mouth to mine. Within the next instant, our tongues are tangling, dueling and sucking. There are certain places on her body where her scent is richer, undiluted, and headier. Here, her mouth. That shadowed valley between her breasts. The spot where torso meets hip. The drenched, sweet haven of her pussy.

I can't get enough. I could feast on her forever and still suffer hunger pains.

Bending, I cup the back of her thighs and hike her up. Her legs wind around my waist, heels locking at the small of my back. Our mouths still partake of each other as I guide us to the office/break room. Carefully, I sit her on the tabletop and attack her coat. As soon as it's on the floor, I go for her scrubs top, leaving her in a T-shirt. But before I can rid her of that, too, she leans back, and goes for the metal snap closure on my overalls.

We both tear the sleeves down my arms, and I have my T-shirt up and over my head in record time. Same with hers. Leaving both of us bare from the waist up except for her bra. And, with a quick snap to the clasp between her breasts, even that barrier is gone.

A groan travels up from my gut and out of me. Goddamn, these tits. I palm them, swooping in for another searing kiss while I skim my thumbs over the beaded nipples. Circling them. Flicking them. I eat up her whimper, silently demand another by pinching those fat tips, tweaking them. And she gives it to me.

Her fingers tighten in my hair, jerking my head back. I

growl my displeasure at that, because I'm not even close to being finished with that mouth.

"What do you need?" she breathes. Turning the tables on me, giving me back my words. And asking me what no one has bothered to before. No one.

My lungs seize, and for a dizzying moment, it's almost as if I'm having an asthma attack. I can't breathe past the constriction. My heart works overtime, and black and gold spots dance at the edges of my vision. But just as suddenly as the sense of suffocation sweeps over me, it disappears, and air painfully rushes back into me.

"Axel." Her fingers massage my scalp, tugging me close until our lips are a breath apart. "What do you need from me? Whatever it is, just ask."

I'm more naked than I've ever been in my life, even though I'm still wearing jeans under my overalls and boots on my feet. But staring into her honeyed gaze, I trust her not to reject me. Not to… leave me.

"Kiss me." I tap my mouth. "Here. Slow."

She leans forward the scant distance separating us to take my mouth, and she makes love to it. Sexes it. Her tongue sweeps in, licking at mine, entwining with it, seducing it, inviting it to play, to dance.

By the time she pulls away, my chest is pumping hard, rising and falling so fast, so hard, the air rushing out of my lungs explodes like grenades between us.

"Here." I point to my neck. *Mark me as yours.* "Don't be gentle," I mimic her from the first time we were together.

Heat, amusement and something else—something softer, more tender—flashes in her eyes, before she lowers her lashes, bends her head and latches on to me. Her teeth graze my throat, and a groan escapes me as that promise of the sweetest edge of pain races straight to my cock. She comes through on that vow. Sinking her teeth into me, she bites down, sucking, bringing her tongue into play, branding me without even being told. Maybe she needs that as much as I do. Needs others to know she's been there as much as I want them to know I've been hers.

God, I hope so.

Delivering one last, luxurious lick up my neck, she hums and nuzzles the base of my throat.

"Here."

This time, I don't point, I tunnel my fingers through all that thick, beautiful hair and show her. Guide her to one nipple. Let her nip, tease, draw, and suckle. Then lead her to the other. Allow her to repeat the same torture. By the time she brings her fingers into play and twists the damp, small tip while raking her teeth over the other, I'm gritting my teeth and wondering how I'm going to survive this without reverting to the base animal that howls and claws at me from the inside.

"Tell me." Her panting bathes my skin. "Anything."

"Lie back."

She shakes her head, biting her bottom lip, and unable to help myself, I thumb it loose. "This is about you—"

"Then lie back." Cupping the front of her neck, I gently squeeze. "Please."

Her breath catches, chest rising, and she arches into my hold. Does she even realize what she's asking me for? As those eyes go hooded until only a narrow band of golden-brown is visible, I know the answer.

Yes. Yes, she does. I give it to her.

My fingers tighten just a fraction, and her moan vibrates against my palm even as she reclines on the table, her hand coming up to clasp my wrist. Her back bows, those gorgeous tits pointing toward the ceiling—taunting me, daring me to taste, to feast.

And I have no control when it comes to her.

But there's something I want more. Something my mouth is watering for. My gut is damn near cramping for a taste of.

Releasing her throat, I quickly remove her trainers then jerk her scrubs and underwear off, tossing them to the floor.

Jesus, she's beautiful. So fucking beautiful.

As lightly as my rough hands can manage, I encircle her ankles, placing them on the edge of the table. Spreading her wide for my hungry gaze. So wet. All that bare, brown and pink flesh drenched and glistening for me.

For me.

Chest filling with more than just air, I release my hold on her throat and bend to her, burying my face in the sweetest, softest place on this earth. Her sharp cry bounces off the grey walls of the room, almost as lovely as the clit I'm strumming. Clamping her writhing hips down, I devour her, granting her no mercy, no quarter. I'm too starved, too desperate, having gone too long without her. A whole twelve hours.

I dip my head and, flattening my tongue, trail the path between her folds, pausing to suck one and then the other. There's no part of her that I don't pay proper homage to, because she deserves it. This is the only gift I have for this warrior queen, and I'm not holding back.

Lust is a grinding wheel in my chest, my gut, and my

cock throbs, roars with the hot rush of blood. And pushing two fingers into her tight, quivering pussy only ups the ante of when I'm going to shame myself by blowing like a green kid with his first sight of a tit. As her slick muscles squeeze me, I shudder, my balls drawing up tight, and yeah, coming all over the back of my zipper is a definite possibility.

"Axel," Zenobia whines, her fingernails scraping my scalp, pussy humping my face. "Please. Inside me. I want you inside me."

I want her to gush over my fingers—long for that pretty clit to tremble and flinch against my tongue, but in all things, her needs supersede mine.

Pulling free of her, I hoist her off the table and flip her face down on the top, that perfect arse up in the air. My eyes not leaving her, I shove my overalls down, followed by my jeans. Moving forward, I cover her, my chest pressed to her back. My face buried in her neck. My fingers tangled with hers.

Though my dick pounds with the need to be balls-deep inside her, I wait, savoring the beauty of our differences. My large frame to her petite build. My angles to her curves. My paleness to her darkness. My vulnerability to her strength.

She's the perfect foil to all that I am, and it humbles me.

Physically shaking my head, as if the gesture can rid it of those fanciful thoughts, I lean back, stroking my palms down the elegant length of her spine. Grasping her rounded hips, I kick her feet wider apart, and because the gnawing greed won't allow me to wait any longer, I plunge inside her pussy.

Our mated groans rent the air, and I still.

Fuck. This pussy.

I've been inside her countless times since that infamous text, and impossibly, each time is like the first. Still tight. Still liquid fire. Still heaven and hell. Still bliss and torture.

Still the answer to every whispered prayer and unspoken dream.

We haven't used condoms since that first day. She's on the pill, and we're both clean. And after having been inside her bareback, strapping back up again after experiencing her without any barrier would've been a little painful. But I would've, because in the end it's her choice. Still, I might've shed a tear when she agreed to go without. This, having nothing between us, is blasphemous joy.

I groan. Dammit. I don't want to move, but damn, I *have* to.

"Ready, pet?"

She nods, and I cover her once more, reaching above her to grasp her fingers and curl them around the edge of the table.

"I've…" I grind my teeth together, willing the words to go back down my throat. But they don't listen. "Missed you."

Even though she's stretched out on the table, her body still tenses. But after a moment, it relaxes, and she nods again. "Missed you, too."

It's soft, almost too soft, but I catch it. The admission shoves into my chest, wraps around my heart, squeezes, and my breath stutters.

Just my asthma making another appearance. That's all it is.

My grip on her hardens, and I pull free, my cock dragging over trembling muscles that set alone almost send my hurtling over into the abyss. My stare is fixed on my flesh and the thick wetness coating it.

Slowly, I sink back inside her, watching as her pussy swallows me whole. After that first pause where she becomes accustomed to me all over again, she takes me so good. Like she was created for me. Like she can't get enough of me. And from the grunts, the dirty grinding, and pleas to "fuck her", she can't.

This woman. She unleashes something feral in me. And as I hike a knee up on the table, spreading that pretty pussy wider, plowing it harder, deeper, all I want is to mark it, mold it so she will never be satisfied by anyone who comes after me. So she will always crave me.

Always come back to me.

"Axel, I need—" She breaks off, lowering an arm and arching up to reach between her and the table to touch her clit.

"Put it back." The order is blunt, sharper than intended, but I'm more animal than man, and in this moment, she's my mate. And I'm responsible for her pleasure. "I got what you need."

Clamping one hand on the nape of her neck, I hook an arm around her neck, find that fat button of flesh and strum it, rub it… pinch it. She chokes on a cry, the tortured sound like a love ballad that strokes down my spine, my arse, to the soles of my feet, then arrows to my balls and cock. That pussy strangles my dick as she comes, soaking me, milking me, hauling me toward my own end.

And I go, a willing sacrifice.

My hand leaves her neck and wraps around her waist, hugging her to my chest, even as I don't let up on her clit, even as I continue to pound her sex. I fuck her. I embrace her.

I need her.

I die a little for her.

And as I come crawl back up from the abyss, broken and bruised and so fucking free, it's her arms that surround me.

A peace that's as foreign to me as this country fills me as we stumble back to the chair, her cuddled on my lap. We don't speak for several minutes, and that's okay, because for some reason, I can't seem to catch my breath. She plays with the ends of my hair while I quietly draw in a deep breath. Or try to. But the wheeze that I am very familiar with rattles in my chest and my ears.

And because she's a nurse—and her ear is pressed to my chest—she catches it.

"Axel." She straightens, frowning, studying my face. "What's wrong?"

"Nowt." But the shortness of breath it's said on ruins the veracity of it. "Just asthma. I have an inhaler. Nowt to worry about."

"Where is it?"

She scrambles off me. And I stand, tugging my jeans and coveralls up, then retrieving my inhaler from my pocket. She quickly dresses but keeps her gaze on me as I take two puffs on it. But unlike earlier, it's not easing the constriction in my chest. A bolt of panic crackles through me, but I forcefully shove it away.

"How're you feeling?" She comes to me again, leaning

close, listening to my chest. When she tilts her head back, the concern on her face hasn't disappeared. "It doesn't sound any better. Is the inhaler not working?"

"Sometimes, I need to take it again." Which I do. And wait. And it feels a little better. Thank fuck. But then I'm coughing again, and it's tighter, not as wet. The wheezing not as loose. And the panic returns. Because I've had asthma since I was a child, and I know the signs. Yet, I suck on the inhaler again. Two more times. Two more times. I don't need to glance at the back of the dispenser to see the counter on zero, even though there would be a reserve of at least ten more doses.

"Axel, we should probably go to the emergency room so you can get a breathing treatment." Her voice took on a clinical quality that makes my skin crawl with humiliation. Moments ago, I was the man fucking her, making her cry out in pleasure, and now I'm a weak patient.

The whistling of my air echoes in my ears, and my chest is beginning to ache, but I grab up my T-shirt and sweep it from the floor and drag it on.

"No." Fuck, why did that have to come out so goddamn feeble? "I'm fine."

"You're obviously not," she snaps.

"Let it go, Zenobia." I stumble over to my welding table, but even that's an effort and has my breathing even more labored, my chest pumping even harder to provide air I don't have. Shit. *Fuck.*

"Screw this." She snatches up her purse. In seconds she has her cell phone out and to her ear. "Yes, this is Zenobia Hester. I'm a nurse at Memorial. I'm with a thirty year-old male experiencing a severe asthma attack. He's used an Albuterol inhaler. Six puffs."

She gives the person on the other end the address of the workshop, coming to kneel beside me. I block her voice out, her scent out.

I concentrate on trying to breathe.

That way, I can also keep the anger and humiliation at bay too.

Just... fuck.

CHAPTER 15

AXEL

"Now tell me again how things are strictly platonic between you and Zenobia." Julian peers down at me, hands tucked into his white doctor's coat. His hazel eyes narrow on me, but it's not irritation or anger darkening them. It's concern.

I get it. He was on duty when the ambulance brought me in, so that had to be a bit of a… surprise. Still, I don't answer. More specifically, I can't. Because I'm currently sucking on the nozzle end of a nebulizer.

Which Julian is using to his advantage.

"I'm sure the dirt on her scrubs and the severe case of sex hair she's sporting could've come from scrambling up in the ambulance, but somehow I doubt it." He props a shoulder against the wall, crossing his arms and ankles. "And then there's the hickey on your neck. But maybe that damn driver hit a pothole and you hit the gurney wrong.

Or you got a little kinky with one of your tools?" He arches a brow.

I return the gesture.

And for the British, the one action can say a lot. For instance, his is current asking, *What do you have to say for yourself, mate?*

And mine is saying, Go fuck yourself.

We're quite multipurpose in our language, us British.

Julian sighs. "Christ, Axel, have you thought this through?"

He pushes off the wall and paces across the room.

"What am I asking?" he barks out a laugh. "You've been thinking with your dick, and yet last time we talked on the phone, you assured me you weren't letting the little head take charge. But maybe if you hadn't, you wouldn't be here in the fucking ER." He pulls my inhaler out of his pocket. "Zero, mate. Zero. And you told me to mind my business last time we talked. What the hell? If Zenobia hadn't been there tonight, would you even have come to the hospital?"

I don't reply again. And not because of the nebulizer. An answer isn't needed because we both know it.

"Shit." He runs his hand over his bald head, and the gesture should be titled Axel is My Pain in the Arse. "Before I forget." He rubs the same hand over his face, glancing at me out of the corner of his eyes.

Unease creeps through me. This is different from his previous browbeating. He's hesitating, and whatever this is, he doesn't want to deliver this news.

"I called your mum to let her know what happened. I wanted to let you know just in case she calls you later."

He doesn't continue—but he doesn't need to. That

silence tells me everything he won't. I can just imagine how that phone call went.

I don't know what to do about him, Julian. What is wrong with him?

He's nothing like Blake, is he?

Why can't he be more like you? Like Blake? I just don't understand him.

It's nothing she hasn't said to me before in another version or fashion.

"No worries. She won't call," I croak. The nebulizer hisses as the last of the Albuterol passes through the tubing. Julian crosses over, takes the nozzle from me and switches off the machine.

Going into doctor mode, he removes his stethoscope from around his neck and orders me to take deeps breaths while he listens to my lungs. "Better. But I think you could do with one more."

He quickly steps outside, speaks with a nurse, then returns, closing the door behind him.

"She's your mum, and she's concerned about you. Of course, she'll call." He states that like it's fact. Like one has any correlation to the other. Like he knows what the fuck he's talking about.

"No," I grind out, "she won't. It's Tuesday, isn't it? Bridge night."

"Axel—"

"Julian, do me a favor, yeah? Fucking shut it."

His mouth flattens, and he glares at me. The only thing probably keeping me from getting my arse handed to me is that I'm already in a hospital bed. But I can't focus on that. Not when pain that has nothing to do with my sore chest is ripping through me.

I shouldn't give a fuck. This isn't the first time my mum or dad have let me know how much of an enigma I am to them at best, a goddamn disappointment of a son, at worst. Their feelings aren't a secret. So why am I sitting here, gutted by her utter failure to give a fuck?

And if my own parents can't be bothered, don't think I'm worth a fucking phone call when I'm sitting in damn hospital, what makes me think others can? Julian? Trish?

Zenobia?

I was fucking fooling myself in the workshop tonight. They all leave. My parents essentially did after Blake's death. As did Julian and Trish, and they'll disappear out of my life again once my gallery show is over. My ex did when she realized I couldn't be the man she needed.

And Zenobia? I only have to give her time. Shit, our temporary relationship was established on walking away from one another, and she's never said anything about changing the terms of that original agreement. Only stupid me wanted more. Dared to think I could have more. Well, I've been reminded that's not possible.

Not for me.

If there's one thing I've learned over and over, it's that alone is better than hurt and rejected. Alone is better than being teased with the promise of love, an end to the loneliness, only to have it ripped away.

Alone is better than bitter hope.

A knock resounds on the door before it opens, and Zenobia pokes her head around the corner.

"Hey, I have the Albuterol you asked for." She enters, closing the door behind her. After handing it to Julian, she shifts closer to me, resting a hand on my forearm. "How're you feeling? Better?"

I move my arm out from under her touch. Because it hurts too much. It reminds me of what I had only an hour ago. Of what I stupidly allowed myself to consider to be mine.

It reminds me of what I would only eventually lose.

"I'm fine. You don't have to stick around because of me. You're off work."

She frowns, glances over at Julian, who is pretending to be incredibly occupied with the nebulizer. "I don't mind. I can give you a ride home. It's not a problem."

"It is for me. I don't need your help. Go home."

Behind her, Julian growls, and behind my rib cage, my heart squeezes hard. I'm wondering if now I'm having a heart attack on top of the asthma. Everything inside me roars at me to stop this, to not be a bloody fool, but something strong—that primal self-protective instinct that is more animalistic than human—has taken control. I'm running, scared, battling for my life, and because of it, I'm scrapping in the mud like the dirtiest street fighter.

"Axel," she whispers, her gaze roaming my face before settling on my gaze.

I can guess what she sees. I've practiced this carefully blank, cold expression for years. It's the only way I've survived the emotionally barren home of my childhood.

"What's going on?"

"I'm thanking you for your help, and I'm saying goodbye. Isn't that what we agreed on? No strings? No demands? No regrets? And it ends when you leave the house. What else is there to discuss?"

"Is this because I called an ambulance?" she rasps, her hand lifting toward me, but when I flinch, she blanches and lowers it back to her side.

Julian hisses, reaching for her, but she sidesteps him, too.

Inside, I'm cracking right down the middle. And grief, as if someone has died, is pouring out of me. But I hold firm. I *have* to.

"This isn't you, and I deserve a better explanation than you reading the terms of our agreement back to me like some contract. For the last time, what the hell. Is. Going. On? And you need to tell me before I turn around and walk out of here and don't come back."

I stare at her. And don't say a word.

Her chin hikes up. Fire flashes in her honey brown eyes —not banked by the glistening of tears.

"Okay, if this is what you want. But I have something to say first."

A fierce light of battle enters her gaze, and once more I'm reminded of the Amazon I called her.

"You're a coward. For not being upfront with me. For using our bargain as a shield to hide behind because you can't be honest with me. You're running scared. And it's not being scared that makes you a coward, Axel. We're all scared. What I feel for you in such a short amount of time fucking terrifies me. No, it's that instead of confronting it, you choose to hurt me. To push me away to save yourself. That makes you a coward." She shakes her head. "I'm sorry I can't hold to those terms I made the mistake of laying out. Because I do have regrets. I regret that I believed you were someone who you obviously aren't. I regret that I betrayed myself *again* and opened my heart to someone. To you. I regret that I trusted you not to hurt me. I regret *you*."

Her words land on me like body blows, pile driving into flesh and bone. Leaving me a battered, bruised, and bloody mess long after she disappears through the door.

"You are a rank bastard." Julian slaps on the nebulizer and thrusts the nozzle at me.

I avoid looking at him like the coward I am, not desiring to see the disgust on his face. The disgust that is etched into my skin.

"How could you do that to her? You fucking know what she's been through with her ex, and you pull that shit? I thought better of you, Axel. You *are* better than that."

I let loose a hollow, bitter laugh. "Apparently not."

"That's utter shit, too. I know you—"

"The fuck you do," I damn near shout, the nebulizer in my hand ignored. "You don't know me, Julian. Other than I'm Blake's brother, who am I? Other than your fucking pet project that you've taken on out of a twisted sense of guilt and obligation. If I didn't share Blake's DNA, you wouldn't even be bothered with me. The *real* me. The antisocial, rude bastard whose own parents only see as the son that should've drowned."

Julian flinches, rocking back on his heels. "Axel."

But I'm too far gone. His call with Mum. Hurting Zenobia. I'm lancing a festering wound, and I can't stop.

"To you, I'm a debt owed, not a person. I don't need your pity, Julian. I don't need you or anyone. So just leave me the fuck alone."

The harsh, labored bursts of my breaths scour the air, and we stare at each other. I don't know how I can be so empty and packed with such rage and pain at the same time. I want to… I want to…

"Breathe." Julian pushes the nebulizer toward me. "Breathe in."

He waits for me to wrap my lips around the end of the nozzle and then heads toward the door.

"You're wrong, y'know," he says, his hand on the knob. "You were always more. You still are."

He opens and leaves.

And I'm alone.

Just like I asked.

CHAPTER 16

AXEL

'm a miserable fuck.

There's no getting around that.

Stepping out of the loo, I scrub the towel over my head, face, and body. And against my will, I glance at my silent phone. Who am I hoping will call? Mum? Zenobia?

Both have equal chances of happening.

Zero.

Rubbing at my chest, I stare at it hard, as if willing it to ring. But it remains stubbornly silent. And the heaviness weighing my sternum down doesn't lessen in the slightest.

I returned to Julian's house from hospital last night with orders to stay away from the workshop for a couple of days. So bolting there is out of the question. But at some point during the early morning hours while staring up at the ceiling, it hit me that I need to stop being a rank coward. I've used art as my escape hatch, my hiding place for so long that it's become a habit. I've become comfortable with it and made excuses for avoiding my parents, Julian, the world.

You're running scared. And it's not being scared that makes you a coward… No, it's that instead of confronting it, you choose to hurt me. To push me away to save yourself. That makes you a coward.

Zenobia's words haunt me as pull on a pair of jeans and a T-shirt. They struck me hard and clawed their way deep because she's right. And not just about her. If I'm brutally honest, I've done the same—pushed people away—with others. Just look at last night with Julian. I lashed out like a wounded animal. If I can't make it good with Zenobia, I can with him. He's been the one person in my life who hasn't left me.

Yet.

After last night, I'm not sure I can say that. But I need to find him and apologize. Fear is a leaden weight in my gut, but I leave the flat and head toward the kitchen entrance. Since he worked the later shift at hospital, I'm hoping he's here. Because this newfound bravery? It might have an expiration date. Like twenty minutes.

The kitchen is empty, and I nearly stumble to a stop, the hollow ache in my chest like a solid punch. For the first morning since I arrived in the States, in this house, there's no Zenobia. And the loneliness that had throbbed like a toothache until this moment yawns into a mortal injury.

I push through the kitchen on bare feet and move into the living room. And find Julian reclined on the couch, a cup of coffee and saucer balanced on his flat stomach and *Grey's Anatomy* on the television.

"You know George dies, right?"

He flicks a glance at me.

"Yeah, hit by a semi. Such an undignified way to go out." He arches an eyebrow. "Let me guess. You got roped into girls' night?"

When I nod, he snickers, then a moment later, sobers.

"How are you feeling?"

"Better."

Nodding, he raises his cup to his mouth and sips. "Are you going to follow doctor's orders and rest for the next couple of days?"

"Yeah." I scrub a hand over my beard and drop in a chair next to the couch. "Can we talk?"

He eyes me, shifting his cup and saucer to the coffee table in front of him and sitting straight. "You? I don't know. Can you?"

His teasing smirk steals the sting out of the ribbing words, and that tight thing squeezing the hell out of my ribs relaxes a fraction. "I'm going to give it my best shot, mate."

At "mate," Julian's eyes widen, and I sigh, dropping my elbows onto my thighs.

"I'm sorry." I laugh, and it's rusty to my ears and throat. "I probably need to be more specific for what, yeah? First, I've been a dick. You were kind enough to invite me to stay here in your home with your family, and I've been an ungrateful ass. I'm sorry for that. And I apologize for last night."

It requires a lot to maintain his gaze, but I do. Because this man, who has been a better friend to me than any other person in my life, deserves that much.

"Zenobia was right when she called me out on my shit.

I'm using this as an excuse, but I've become so accustomed to not measuring up to who I believed people wanted me to be, that I used it as a wall to keep people out. To push them away before they could reject me. That's what I did with you and Trish. In my mind, as soon as you felt your debt to Blake was paid in full, you wouldn't want anything to do with me. So I distanced myself first. Only you refused to go away."

I shake my head.

"Part of me was afraid to come here. Because I believed the more time you spent around me, the faster you would realize I wasn't worth your trouble and you'd finally reach that breaking point. And I'd lose the one person who hadn't given up on me."

I swallow hard past the constriction in my throat. Admitting that truth that I'd just now acknowledged to myself—my fear of losing Julian, of having him see me as unworthy—was difficult.

And liberating.

"Last night, at the hospital, with you seeing how weak I was, how much of a burden I could be, I panicked. And I resorted to what has become a pattern for me. I hurt you, Julian. And I'm sorry."

He bows his head, studying his loosely clasped fingers between his thighs. "Thank you for that. It took a lot for you to come find me and say it." Another few moments of silence beats between us before he leans back and looks at me. "But it wasn't necessary. I forgave you last night. When I said I knew you, those weren't just words. I meant them. You might believe I've remained in contact with you all these years because of my friendship with

Blake—and yes, that's part of it—but it's not the whole reason."

He rises with a heavy sigh, crossing over to the big window on the other side of the living room. Standing in front of it, he stares out over the front yard, his back to me.

"Before Blake died, he would sneak your drawings out of your room and show them off to Trish and me, because he knew you were much too shy to share them with anyone. God, he was so proud of you. Where most big brothers found their younger brothers annoying, that wasn't the case with you. He genuinely adored you and bragged about how brilliant and gifted you were. And when he died..." His voice thickens on those last two words, and my throat tightens in sympathy.

Then Julian clears his throat, his shoulders straightening.

"When he died, I lost a best friend, but you lost a brother. And true, Blake would've wanted me to watch out for you, but Axel, you have it all wrong."

Julian turns around, and the stark emotion—pain, grief, love—etching his face has me rising to my feet. "The way Blake loved you, the way he saw you, it wasn't you who should've been worried about measuring up. I was afraid—have always been afraid—that *I* wasn't good enough *for you*. I've been scared I failed you. Because you deserve better."

Shock petrifies me. Nothing and *everything* roll through my head in a deafening roar. How could successful, smart, proud Julian Arliss feel unworthy of *me*? It doesn't make sense. And my mind can't wrap around it.

"Axel." Julian recrosses the room and stops in front of

me. "I'm sorry too. Because instead of thinking you knew that my actions spoke for themselves, I should've told you all of this before. Starting now, let me make it abundantly clear. I love you. Not like a brother. Because to me, you *are* my brother."

He hauls me into his arms.

His tight embrace cracks the ice on my paralysis, and I hug him back. Just as tightly. Just as fiercely.

As a brother.

"I love you, too."

CHAPTER 17

glance down as an elbow knocks against mine, and Bethany tips her head back, smiling up at me as we and her parents step outside of Roger Williams Park Zoo. This isn't my first trip to the small zoo south of downtown Providence, and apparently it isn't hers either. By far. But it's one of her favorite places in the city, and she wanted to spend a couple of hours with me here.

When Bethany, with Danielle and Gregory's permission, called a couple of days ago and invited me to meet them here, I leaped on it. After the breakup—can I call, really call it a breakup when, technically, we weren't together in the first place?—with Axel four days earlier, I desperately needed the distraction. Even the controlled chaos of the emergency department hadn't provided enough of one to totally evict him from my mind. And, though I love them, having Gabrielle and Julian back haven't helped either. It's required every tattered and tested scrap of pride I have not to ask about him.

But I haven't done it.

Yet.

This week, I've held on.

Next week is another matter.

Because it seems like in the battle between pride and love, there aren't any clear winners, and the outcome is muddy as fuck.

Jesus, leave it to me to fall in love with an emotionally and geographically unavailable man in a number of days. Like some really sappy and bad romance novel. And not even the good sappy, bad ones where there's a happily ever after or happily ever after for now. Nope, the awful novels where the hero dies or falls for the heroine's best friend, and the heroine is writing about that shit thirty years later in a dusty journal.

Except, no one's died.

It's just felt like it.

Oh, for fuck's sake, falling in love with Axel has turned me into a maudlin, depressing bitch who is getting on my own damn nerves.

I hate love.

I hate men who look like Vikings with ice blue eyes, tattoos, and wounded souls.

I hate that I'm lying.

"Did you have a good time, Z?" Bethany nudges me again.

Even though my heart is aching, and my chest feels like someone reached in and snatched out a vital part of me, leaving me rattling and hollow, I summon up a smile.

Honestly, for her, it's no hardship at all. Looking at her brings me joy.

"I sure did. Your mom told me you like to come here and sketch the snakes." I over-exaggerate a shudder. But only a little. Those things are evil as fuck. "Brave girl."

"I do. Getting down all the details in their scales and eyes is fun and a challenge." She grins, and it strikes me as a little wicked. "What's the matter? Don't tell me you're afraid of the snakes?" She snickers. "I might've noticed you hiding behind my dad."

"A healthy respect for them. Not fear."

"And she wasn't hiding, Bethany," Gregory adds, sliding an arm around her shoulders and squeezing. "You were just taking in the aerial view, right, Zenobia?"

"Exactly." I nod and return his grin.

There have been surprisingly easy moments between the Mavises and me through the day. Not a lot of them. Our —well, relationship is too strong a word—alliance is too new to enjoy a true camaraderie. There's also still a sense of… possessiveness they have over their daughter when it comes to me. And I get it. As much as Bethany must have assured them about only wanting to get to know me as a friend, they probably still feel a little threatened about my intrusion into their lives. Fingers crossed, the more time we spend together, the easier it will become for them. At least I hope so.

Because I want her in my life.

"We should head home," Danielle says.

She's going to be the hardest nut to crack. Again, I get it. I didn't come into this expecting miracles. Just a chance. And, I'm grateful for it.

"Ready, sweetheart?"

"Ready, Mom." Bethany smiles at her mother, then turns back to me, throwing her arms around my waist in an impromptu hug that has tears stinging my eyes.

I blink them back as I return the embrace.

"Thanks for coming, Z. I'll text you later, okay?"

"Deal. Make sure you okay it with your parents first, though?"

"Got it." She releases me and grabbing her mother's hand, gives me one last wave, and heads off across the parking lot with them.

I remain at the zoo's entrance for a few extra moments, watching them, gathering myself. This happened. I got to spend the day with my daughter. Blowing out a breath, I will my pulse to slow. At some point, I need to call my mom and let her know about the change of events. It's funny how I shared everything about Bethany—seeing her again, setting up an arrangement to get to know her—with Axel first, but not my own mother. Not that she won't be happy for me. At least I think she will. We haven't spoken about Bethany since I returned from the hospital after giving birth.

Another thing I've decided to own up to since accepting my feelings for Axel. My resentment of my mother and grandparents. I can have lingering anger toward them for not supporting me and still adore them. And it's okay. Because I've forgiven them. The good they've given me and shown me far outweighs a moment we faced when all of us were out of our depth. I can't hold that against them.

A smirk rides my lips as I walk toward my car. I've become a regular Dr. Phil since Axel dumped me. Of course, that might have something to do with me deciding to return to counseling. Since James's betrayal and desertion, I haven't been kind to myself. I've blamed myself for things that aren't my sins, and some of that goes back to getting pregnant and the adoption. There's nothing wrong with a refresher round of counseling, and I deserve to be the healthiest, best me I can be. For Bethany, the Mavises, and for myself.

I press the key fob and glance in the direction of the flashing lights. There I... am...

No.

It can't be.

But as Axel pushes off the side of my car and stalks my way, I can't deny that he's a figment of my starved imagination.

Move. Walk past him.

My brain issues the order, but by the time my feet move, it's too late. He's in front of me, his clean cedar scent enveloping me. His beautiful, shockingly blue eyes roam my face as if he's seeing me for the first time in four years instead of days. His blond hair frames those razor-sharp cheekbones, tempting me to trace the blades with my lips before touching them to his waiting mouth.

His long, elegant fingers flex next to his thick, denim-covered thighs as if he's barely controlling himself from reaching for me...

It's those hands that snap me out of my stupor.

Because he might not have used them to shove me out of that hospital room door, but he did it just the same.

"What're you doing here, Axel?" Dammit. Why does my

voice contain a hoarse rasp instead of a strong, what-the-fuck-do-you-want sneer?

"Gabrielle told me you would be here for the first meeting with Bethany and her parents. I wanted to be here just in case you—"

"What? Needed you?" I scoff. *Stop that shit right now,* I scold my traitorous heart as it simultaneously squeezes and sighs. *He wants no part of you. Get your shit together.* "Nope. All good here. If that's it…"

I step forward, but he doesn't move. His hands lift as if to grip my arms, but hell no.

"Don't." I jerk backward, my pulse thudding in my ears.

Jesus, he can't touch me. I'm not fool enough to think that I've developed an immunity to him. That's not possible. And I can't fold in front of him. I might love him, but I've already been in a relationship where I was more invested than the other person. That profit margin cost me too much.

And with Axel?

I would make the stock market crash of 1929 look like a banner day.

I won't sell myself short like that ever again. I'm worth more than that.

"Fine. I won't touch you. I promise." He holds his hands up, palms out, that gruff voice so gentle I want to curl up around it even as I know it's impossible for several reasons. "Just… Two minutes. I don't deserve them, but please give me two minutes and then I won't bother you again."

I don't reply.

But I don't walk away either.

I'm a fool.

"Everything you said in hospital that night… You were right. I was running scared. If I'm honest, I've been running scared since I met you. You are so unlike any woman I've known, and being with you isn't just a night watching TV. Or a night eating Chinese food. Or a night making love. It's an epiphany. An awakening. But when you've been asleep and in self-preservation mode for most of your life, coming alive outside of the one thing that's been your reason for breathing—and for me that's always been art, sculpting—it's terrifying. You terrified me. I don't know how to explain it. But it's like…"

He frowns, his throat working as he glances down, as if searching the ground for the answer. When he returns his gaze to mine, there's a fierceness there that steals what little breath I maintained since he started talking.

"It's like living underwater all your life and never having used your lungs before. And when you break the surface, that first gasp of breath is like fire to your lungs. It's jarring, painful. Scary. But it's also so beautiful that you can never return underwater again. No matter how much you want to return because the familiar is better than the unknown. That's what you are for me, Zenobia. That first lungful of air. And I tried to go back to the world I knew. But it's dark there without you. It's cold. It's lonely. Too quiet. I don't want to be there anymore. I need you. More than you could possibly need me. I need you to be my noise. My color. My pain. My fire. My heartbeat."

He shifts closer and his palm raises, hovers next to my cheek. But he doesn't touch me, respecting my wishes. I note the fine tremble in that hand, and it echoes the one in my heart.

"I love you," he whispers. "And I'm sorry I hurt you to save myself. You were right to call me a coward. But I'm not anymore. I'm still scared as fuck, but I'm willing to be frightened with you. For you. Because I can't be without you. I love you."

Part of me yells that I should let him sweat it out. I should make him suffer. Because he hurt me. And it's true he did. But this man standing in front of me with his heart in his eyes and hands? Yes, he very well might hurt me in the future, but it won't be in the way he did in that ER room, and it won't be intentionally. Because I believe him when he says he loves me.

So, I shut that bitter bitch up and throw myself into his arms.

And he catches me.

Just like I knew he would.

Still… "If you pull that shit again, I'll cut you to the white meat," I snarl, pulling back and jabbing a finger at his nose.

His arms lock around me, frowning as he pulls me tight against him. "Is that an American thing I'm going to have to learn like grits?"

"That and *Real Housewives of Atlanta.*"

"Oh fuck."

I grin. "I love you, too."

And I kiss him.

Because that's what you do when you have a happily ever after.

ACKNOWLEDGMENTS

First and always, thank you to my heavenly Father who has made all of this possible. I've co-written every book with You, and not only can I not do it without You, I don't want to!

To Gary. Thank you for being the most amazing husband, partner, cheerleader, chef and rock. You are my real-life hero, and I love you now and forever.

To Dahlia Rose or my writing partner-in-crime. Our writing challenges and your many ear worms have gotten me through many books, including this one. I am so blessed to call you friend.

To Kenya Goree-Bell. I don't think you know how much I appreciate your friendship, your belief in me and your huge, beautiful, glittery rainbow spirit. If not for you, I might still be writing this book. Thank you for the kick in the pants and the advice. You're my girl, and not only do I adore you, I love you. See? There. It's in print. You can never deny that I've said it! LOL!

To Debra Glass for being my mentor, friend and critique partner after all these years. We're still going strong! And I'm still asking, How does she KNOW THESE THINGS? LOL! You never cease to amaze me with your selflessness and knowledge.

A huge thank you to Talia Hibbert for helping me with

shape Axel into the growly, proper—but not too proper—British hero I imagined. I so appreciate the time and patience you gave me in answering all of my questions and emails. You exemplify the kindness that is in this industry.

To Michel Prince. Thank you SO much for not having me out here in these publishing streets sounding like a Grey's Anatomy reject! LOL! You went over and beyond answering all of my numerous medical questions, and you have no idea how grateful I am for your patience and generosity of knowledge. You rock, woman!

And finally, a ginormous thank you to the Saints and Sinners. Your enthusiasm for this book kept me going, and I just love all of you! Thank you for giving me a safe space to let my freak flag fly! LOL!

ABOUT NAIMA SIMONE

USA Today Bestselling author Naima Simone's love of romance was first stirred by Johanna Lindsey, Sandra Brown and Nora Robert's many years ago. Well not that many. She is only eighteen…ish. Though her first attempt at a romance novel starring Ralph Tresvant from New Edition never saw the light of day, her love of romance, reading and writing has endured. Published since 2009, she spends her days—and nights—creating stories of unique men and women who experience the first bites of desire, the dizzying heights of passion, and the tender, healing heat of love.

She is wife to Superman, or his non-Kryptonian, less bullet proof equivalent, and mother to the most awesome kids ever. They all live in perfect, sometimes domestically-challenged bliss in the southern United States.

Visit Naima at www.naimasimone.com. Or connect with Naima through email (nsimonebooks@aol.com), through her website, through her newsletter or become a member of her fabulous Facebook Street Team.

ALSO BY NAIMA SIMONE

Fairy Tales Unleased

Bargain with the Beast

A Perfect Fit

Love on the Radio

Jessie's Girl

Don't You Forget About Me

Please Don't Go, Girl

Secrets and Sins Series

Gabriel

Malachim

Raphael

Chayot

Guarding Her Body Series

Witness to Passion

Killer Curves

Bachelor Auction Series

Beauty and the Bachelor

The Millionaire Makeover

The Bachelor's Promise

A Millionaire at Midnight